# A FAVORITE DAUGHTER

## A PRIDE AND PREJUDICE VARIATION

## P. O. DIXON

**A Favorite Daughter**

*A Pride and Prejudice Variation*

Copyright © 2020 by P. O. Dixon

ISBN-13: 9798625806282

*To readers, all around the world, who enjoy my Pride &*
*Prejudice Variations.*

# CONTENTS

## ACKNOWLEDGMENTS

Heartfelt gratitude is bestowed to Miss Jane Austen for her timeless classic, *Pride and Prejudice*, which makes all this possible.

What a joy it is imagining different paths to happily ever after for our beloved couple, Darcy and Elizabeth, and then sharing the stories with the world.

Special thanks for all you do, Betty and Deborah.

# INTRODUCTION

Written in the tradition of many other P. O. Dixon *Pride and Prejudice* retellings, this charming story combines familiar elements of Jane Austen's classic to satisfy your want of nostalgia and lots of delightful twists throughout to quench your desire for another romantic escape with Darcy and Elizabeth.

*A Favorite Daughter* begins in Hertfordshire amid the aftermath of Mr. Thomas Bennet's passing.

Mr. Bennet had very often wished that, instead of spending his whole income, he had laid by an annual sum for the better provision of his children, and of his wife, if she survived him.

Alas, he did not live long enough to do it.

After her father's untimely death, Miss Elizabeth Bennet reads a letter from him in which he tasks her with the protection of her family.

Elizabeth is willing to do everything in her power to fulfill her father's dying wish, even if it means marrying a man she cannot love.

There is, however, one man whom she can love. Mr. Fitzwilliam Darcy. The two start out as friends, but Mr. Darcy wants more. Much more.

Surely Elizabeth will not always sacrifice her own happiness for the sake of her family. Or will she?

***

**Author's Note:** This heartwarming story is a *Pride and Prejudice* retelling designed to do just that, to warm your heart and add a bit of joy along the way. Nothing more and certainly nothing less. All the best!

"That the wish of giving happiness to you might add force to the other inducements which led me on, I shall not attempt to deny."

— JANE AUSTEN

# PROLOGUE

*I*f you are reading this letter, my dearest Lizzy, it means you have not preceded me in death. Therefore, I must insist you do not mourn ever long for me. Things are just as they ought to be.

Indeed, this is one area in life in which I have succeeded. No parent wishes to outlive a most beloved child.

If only I might boast of such success in other endeavors—most notably begetting a son to inherit Longbourn. Do I do you a disservice, my child, in contenting myself with the notion that you are like the son I never had? I think not.

Please know that were it in my power to change the terms of the entail, I most assuredly would have done so. I would have bequeathed our family's home and all my worldly possessions to you.

No one is more deserving.

*Instead, I have left you with the unenviable task of caring for your mother, your sisters, and, most importantly, yourself. Were the burden to fall to a lesser person, I might have great cause for concern. That is not to say I believe you will not be met with more than your share of challenges. When trying times come, as they inevitably will, I ask you to embrace your own sage philosophy.*

*Remember, your courage always rises with any attempts to intimidate you.*

*Yours in eternal life,*
*Thomas Bennet*

## CHAPTER 1

HERTFORDSHIRE, ENGLAND – SPRING 1812

The son her father never had, indeed. Miss Elizabeth Bennet bore this depiction of herself with pride. Being her late father's favorite daughter, she had shouldered all his estate-related responsibilities, for all intents and purposes. Not that she had not met with more than her share of resistance over the past year, what with the estate's solicitors being unwilling to work with a lowly female. Her uncle, Mr. Phillips, a local attorney who lived in the nearby town of Meryton, had thereby served as her proxy, but it was Elizabeth who made all the decisions.

On that particular day, she met her friend, Charlotte Lucas, from the neighboring estate, in the lane, and decided to turn and walk with her. Despite having four sisters of her own, Elizabeth relished time spent with Charlotte. Though she was Charlotte's junior by at least six years, theirs was the most intimate of friendships.

For the most part, Charlotte was a peaceful, easygoing person. She was also practical—too practical at times from Elizabeth's viewpoint. Charlotte sought comfort even if it meant setting aside her own personal desires. Bent on avoiding conflict and discomfort, she could be accommodating and complacent in a relationship. Elizabeth always felt a particular calm and peacefulness in Charlotte's presence—a much-needed respite of late, what with the never-ending chaos at Longbourn.

"How is Jane getting along this morning?" Charlotte asked.

"She does very well," replied Elizabeth. Jane was the eldest Bennet daughter. Owing to a debilitating illness during childhood, she seldom left Longbourn Village. To that day, it pained Elizabeth to witness her dearest sister's affliction, knowing the limitations inherent in such a state, but Jane bore it with grace and dignity.

"Do give her my best and tell her I look forward to seeing her soon."

"I shall, indeed. And you must extend my felicitations to your family as well."

The other young woman nodded, signaling she would. "Has there been any progress toward locating the heir of Longbourn?" Charlotte continued.

Elizabeth shrugged. "So far as I know, the gentleman's identity and hence his whereabouts remain a mystery."

"That is a shame. I know how heavily the uncertainty must be weighing on all of you."

The situation of the entail on her father's estate had long cast a pall on her family's equanimity, especially that of Elizabeth's mother, Mrs. Fanny Bennet, who fancied herself as being of a nervous constitution. Not a day had passed since Mr. Bennet's death that his widow did not bemoan the helplessness, the injustice, and the cruelty of their fate.

The matter of the missing heir heightened everyone's distress. The gentleman's name was Mr. Robert Cotton. An exhaustive effort to let him know what had happened had been undertaken. He was said to be living on the continent in Spain. Indeed, he had lived there for years, but he had since removed himself to the Americas.

The search, therefore, continued. Some months later, evidence was uncovered that Mr. Cotton had lived in Canada, but he died, leaving no known children. Thus, the next male in line to inherit Longbourn needed to be notified, but first said person needed to be identified and located.

Elizabeth would have been perfectly satisfied if such a person's identity was never uncovered. The nagging thought that a stranger might arrive on Longbourn's doorstep any day, with a wife and children in tow, prepared to toss her own family into the hedgerows, had been her constant companion for the past long months.

"It is such a shame to find oneself always at the mercy of the dictates of the opposite sex," Elizabeth opined.

"Whoever said it is a man's world knew exactly of what he spoke," Charlotte said.

"I should like to think it will not always be this way."

Charlotte shrugged a little. "Perhaps in generations to come, when our daughters' daughters have daughters," she waxed poetic. "But, then again, we must rely upon the opposite sex to have daughters. Must we not?"

Both ladies laughed at this conjecture.

"As much as I am loath to confess it," Charlotte continued, "the odds are not exactly in our favor in that regard as we are both on the wrong side of twenty with nary a prospect in sight. I dare say, however, your chances are not nearly so dire as mine with my being seven and twenty."

"I prefer to think all is not quite lost," Elizabeth said. "Netherfield has remained unoccupied for far too long. Perhaps a wealthy gentleman from town will decide to purchase it, and when he takes possession, he will be accompanied by enough wealthy gentlemen friends that we may have a surfeit of suitors from which to choose."

"No doubt our mothers would be thrilled by such a prospect," Charlotte cried.

"As would we all, I am sure," said Elizabeth, her spirits rising to playfulness. "Who among us is not in want of a single man of a large fortune?"

# CHAPTER 2

LONDON, ENGLAND

*A* moment or two passed before Fitzwilliam Darcy ascended the stairs of his friend Charles Bingley's home.

Despite Charles's being one of his closest friends, Darcy rarely called at Bingley's and with good reason. He would do anything to avoid spending time in company with Bingley's younger sister, Miss Caroline Bingley.

Now there he stood and at the young lady's behest, no less, by means of a trusted servant. She would not say what was the nature of her summons, only that it was of the utmost importance, and it involved Bingley's entire future. As Bingley was always getting himself into one poorly conceived scheme or another, Darcy dropped all he was doing and made his way there.

"Darcy, my friend," said Bingley, bolting from his chair, when Darcy was shown into the drawing-room. "You are just the person whom I wished to see."

"You are just the person we all wished to see," exclaimed Miss Bingley, no doubt speaking on behalf of her brother-in-law and her elder sister, Reginald and Louisa Hurst, who were sitting on the sofa opposite her.

Arising to her feet, Miss Bingley hurried across the room and seizing Darcy by his arm, began coaxing him farther into the room. "It is imperative you speak with my brother, Charles, about what he has done before it is too late!"

"Pay no attention to my sister," said Bingley. "No doubt, once you have heard my news, you will be joining me in a congratulatory toast to my good fortune."

That what was considered positive by Bingley was viewed as negative by Miss Bingley came as no surprise to Darcy. The opposing nature of the two often balanced each other out and allowed the two siblings to coexist together peacefully. What Bingley appreciated most about his sister was her wit, and she, in turn, lauded his amiability. Problems arose when Miss Bingley supposed her concerns for her brother's welfare were being dismissed, and she looked to dampen down her brother's excessive optimism.

In response, Bingley was wont to grow impatient with what he believed was his sister's negativity and attempt to restrain him. This was one such a time.

Darcy knew the siblings too well to dismiss either of their concerns out of hand by siding with one over the other. On the other hand, Bingley was nothing if not impulsive. The older of the two gentlemen, Darcy had been obliged to rescue his friend from quite a few quandaries, owing to the younger man's flightiness.

"Bingley," Darcy said, his voice evidencing some concern, "what have you done?"

"Come, have a seat," Bingley urged. "I shall tell you everything."

"Yes," Miss Bingley added. "You will want to be seated when you hear this."

Bingley rolled his eyes. "As usual, Caroline is over-reacting."

"Who that knows you as well as I do could help but feel the way I do!" She looked at her sister. "Louisa is just as concerned as I am, are you not?"

Louisa's expression was unreadable, which also

came as no surprise to Darcy. Despite always being a staunch supporter of whatever scheme the younger sister concocted, the elder sister did not like finding herself in the middle of disagreements between her siblings. She said nothing.

"Again," Darcy said after taking a seat closest to Bingley, "what have you done?"

Returning to his own seat, Bingley cleared his throat. "Well, you know that my excellent father always intended to purchase an estate."

Indeed, Darcy knew the story well. Bingley had inherited property in the amount of nearly a hundred thousand pounds from his father, who, as his friend cited, had intended to purchase an estate but did not live to do it.

"I have just returned from Hertfordshire," said Bingley in concluding his speech.

"You are looking at the new owner of a long unin-habited estate in some godforsaken part of the country just outside of some small town of which no one has ever heard," Miss Bingley exclaimed.

Darcy caught his breath. *Dear God, pray Bingley has not been duped!*

Darcy dared not voice such a concern out loud. Bingley had the right to spend his fortune in whatever manner he might choose. But he had seen his friend mere days prior, and there had been no mention whatsoever of such grandiose plans.

"Trust me, Darcy, the situation is hardly as dire as Caroline makes it sound."

"Who in the world would purchase an estate on a whim? Who would forgo an exhaustive search of all the other properties to be seen before entering into such an endeavor and without proper counsel, and most of all, who would purchase an estate in the middle of nowhere?" Miss Bingley cried. "Can you really expect our friends and acquaintances from town to travel to the wilds of Hertfordshire for visits?" She peered at Darcy. "Surely you agree with me. Surely you have the same questions."

Sitting on the edge of his seat, his spine straight, Darcy said, "I must confess to wanting to know more."

Bingley said, "It is not as though I did not consider such things. It is just that I took one look at the place, and I knew I was destined to be its master. That said, I did exercise some caution. You see, rather than make an offer to purchase the estate, I decided to let it instead."

That last detail must have been news to Miss Bingley. Her face gradually contorted from wariness to relief.

Darcy released his breath. "Does the estate have a name?"

Bingley nodded. "The name of the estate is Netherfield Park. And the unheard-of town that Caroline spoke of so dismissively is Meryton. I daresay it is roughly the size of Lambton."

The young woman scoffed. "Next, I suppose you will be comparing Netherfield Park to Pemberley, Mr. Darcy's home."

"Netherfield Park is no Pemberley by any stretch of the imagination, but it is perfect for me." Directing his attention to Darcy, he continued, "I can hardly wait to show it to you. I am counting on you to be my guest, and as my closest and most trusted friend, I am hoping you will teach me all there is to know about the management of such an estate."

Between Bingley and Darcy, there was a very steady friendship, in spite of great opposition of character. Indeed, Darcy found Bingley's easiness, openness, and ductility of his temper to be most endearing —a disposition which offered a pronounced contrast to Darcy's own. The older man was clever, reserved, and fastidious, and his manners, though well-bred, were not inviting.

On the strength of Darcy's regard, Bingley had the firmest reliance, and of his judgment, the highest opinion. This was all the more reason for Darcy's concern that Bingley had taken on the responsibility of an estate, even if he was meant to be a tenant.

*Bingley's situation, though impetuously conceived, is salvageable.*

Leaning forward, Darcy extended his hand to his friend. "Bingley, you know I will do whatever I can to be of service to you."

"Capital!" Bingley exclaimed, accepting his friend's show of support. "I plan to return to Netherfield as soon as the manor house is properly situated. Pray, you will be among my party. I really do not think I will enjoy this new adventure half so much as I might unless you are by my side."

# CHAPTER 3

KENT, ENGLAND

*A* man of the cloth, Mr. William Collins knew himself to be an excellent arbiter of that which would be considered a fault. Among his list of human frailties, pride was uppermost. However, on that particular day, he could not help but feel a certain sense of pride owing to his good fortune.

A young man of five and twenty, he came from modest means. During the prior year, he had been granted the living in Hunsford, near Westerham, Kent, by the Right Honorable Lady Catherine de Bourgh. A humble man, by his own estimation, he was thereby set for the rest of his life.

Indeed, he had no reason to suppose his situation in life could get any better than it was. Then, he received notification that he had inherited an estate in Hertfordshire. Located near the small town of Meryton, the estate was named Longbourn Village. Almost overnight, it seemed, he was the master of his own home. He was a landowner. He was a gentleman in every sense of the word. Mr. Collins's happiness was almost complete.

If ever there was a cause to suffer pride, this was it.

Mr. Collins, who had been hurrying along the lane, halted in his tracks. What a splendid view of the manor house he beheld. It was idyllically situated in the heart of Rosings Park. The green grass beneath his feet was as lush as the most exquisite Persian rug. The glazing on the manor house alone, he knew to be quite costly. The sun's rays reflecting off the windows of the manor house gave further proof to the structure's majesty.

He'd spent many hours venturing back and forth between his humble little abode, which abutted the estate, and the manor house. The thought of how many more times he would pass that way again overcame him. Collecting himself, Collins swallowed. Soon enough, he would be standing before his own manor house, admiring all there was to see. This consolation spurred him on, even hastened his pace, for his noble patroness was not one to be kept waiting.

Indeed, Lady Catherine had been the one to summon him as was her wont to do whenever she was in the want of diversion.

What a stroke of luck it was to be summoned on the very day he wished to seek an audience with the grand lady. He needed to share his happy news with his noble patroness who, to his way of thinking, had been the first person to recognize him for the honorable man that he always strived to be throughout his entire life. He did not, however, want to give her the impression that he was not grateful to her. He was sure he would forever be in her debt.

As evidence of his gratitude, he meant to offer to stay on at the parsonage until such time as a new parson could be installed in his place. Whether it be a month, two months, six months, or even a year, his commitment would remain steadfast. He owed everything to Lady Catherine. Besides, he liked to think that his elevated station in life would enhance rather than diminish their connection to each other going forward.

Moments later, the eager gentleman was shown into the drawing-room where her ladyship awaited his arrival. Once all the usual civilities were exchanged, and the tea-things were set, her ladyship wasted no time pressing her point.

Seated in the center of the ornate room in a gilded chair befitting her noble roots, the grand lady looked as though she were holding court. "You can be at no loss, Mr. Collins, to understand the reason I have summoned you here this afternoon. Nothing that happens in this parish escapes my knowing."

Collins had no reason to doubt her ladyship's claim. In the short time that had passed since he assumed his duties, he knew almost everything there was to know about his parishioners. For that, he had Lady Catherine to thank. The business of her life was to be of service to others, and by her own account, no one was more qualified than she was in that regard. Mr. Collins, of course, could not agree more.

"Indeed, Lady Catherine," he began, "I am very aware of your omnipotence as regards all such matters. I am most grateful for the opportunity you have given me to speak with you and, hopefully, to seek your counsel, for it is with a rather conflicted heart that I come before you this afternoon. I hardly know where to start."

"Ordinarily, one would start at the beginning. However, the frankness of my character does not allow me to feign ignorance of your situation." Setting aside her cup, she continued. "I understand that owing to the confirmed demise of the previous heir apparent, you are now the owner of a small, country estate in Hertfordshire."

Mr. Collins nodded. He meant to say something that might aptly convey his sentiments as well as atone for the disruption that was sure to follow, but before he could fashion his response, Lady Catherine said, "If not for the particular circumstances of your good fortune, I would be congratulating you. But the celebration of someone's untimely death–even the death of someone that one does not know–is hardly a cause for joy."

For as much as her ladyship already knew of the inheritance, there was even more to be discovered, and thus a lengthy back-and-forth discussion ensued, during which Collins did more listening than speaking. Soon the matter of Longbourn's current inhabitants arose. Mr. Collins told his inquisitive patroness all he knew. He had almost exhausted himself on the subject when Lady Catherine seized control of the conversation.

"Five daughters!" Lady Catherine exclaimed. "All of them single?"

Mr. Collins's head bobbed two or three times.

Her ladyship rose from her seat. She started pacing

the marble tile floor. "I have heard all I need to hear in order to advise you on what you ought to do. Despite this turn in fortune, you are a man of the cloth, for I believe having been called, it will always be your true calling. You ought to extend your good fortune to the Bennet family.

"I have been meaning to instruct you to choose a wife for some time. It stands to reason that you must choose one of the Bennet daughters. If you do not heed my advice, then what is to become of them? Do you mean to throw the widow and her five single daughters into the hedgerows and thereby render them beholding to sundry family members?"

She ceased pacing and regarded Collins directly. "Did I correctly understand you to say the mother is the daughter of a tradesman? That her daughters have little to no dowries to speak of? I daresay you are that family's best hope."

"Do you really suppose the family might be receptive to such a scheme, your ladyship?"

Not that Collins doubted his ability to woo whichever Bennet daughter he set his cap on, but he knew Lady Catherine well enough to know she would appreciate his modesty. Such false modesty on his part would never do among those whom he considered his equals and most especially among his inferiors. With the incomparable Lady Catherine de Bourgh, diffidence was the order of the day.

In his heart, he knew any woman would fancy herself fortunate to have garnered his affections and never more so than now, what with his being among the landed gentry.

"Do you think I would have proposed the scheme if I suffered a shred of doubt regarding its viability? What choice do they have?" she asked, resuming her former attitude pacing the floor. "Surely they must know they are beholden to you—that you may turn them out as soon as you please.

"It is decided. You must travel to Hertfordshire and make an offer of marriage to one of your Bennet cousins.

"That said, I advise you to choose properly. One must assume the young ladies are all gentlewomen in every sense of the word, despite their recent impoverishment, but one must also suppose they are vastly different in temperament. Choose wisely for my own sake, especially, should there be a possibility of any future connection between us. Choose judiciously for your own sake as well. Let the Bennet daughter of your choice be an active, useful sort of person and one who knows and understands a woman's place. One can only suppose the Bennet daughters were not brought up high, especially with relations in trade."

Steadily pacing, she said, "I do not suppose such an estate as Longbourn allows for any degree of extravagance. No doubt, the Bennets are not accustomed to having much, which will serve you well. If you are to have any chance of getting rid of the other four sisters after you have married the most sensible of them, you will have to be ever mindful of what must be very meager dowries, and you must always be cognizant of ways to supplement them."

Concluding her directive, Lady Catherine said, "Do as I say, and your felicity in marriage shall be assured. As soon as you can, you must bring your bride to Rosings, where I shall be happy to receive her as my guest."

# CHAPTER 4

"Why must one of us be obliged to marry that odious man?" cried the youngest Bennet daughter, Lydia. "It is not as though he is an officer. Perhaps if he were an officer, then none of us would have any cause to repine, for who would not wish to catch such a man?"

Suffice it to say that upon his much-anticipated arrival at Longbourn, Mr. William Collins did not make the most favorable impression on his Bennet relations. No sooner than he had presented himself to the family as a distant cousin and heir of the estate, he requested a private audience with the lady of the house. Having written to Mrs. Bennet the week before, Collins first congratulated himself on his own good fortune even as he apologized for the nature of its being brought about. The gentleman's letter went on to read:

*"Although I am sure nothing can take the place of a most beloved husband and father, as I am certain the late Mr. Thomas Bennet indeed was, I have every intention of making amends for the inconvenience of the entail on the estate afforded to you and your daughters. As I now find myself a single man and the master of an estate, it is incumbent upon me to find a wife. I can think of no greater reparation to your family than to choose a bride from among your five daughters."*

Upon reading these words, Mrs. Bennet hardly attended to anything else he had written. Not only was Collins's letter akin to music to her ears, but it was also an answer to her prayers. The business of Longbourn's missing heir, as well as a preponderance of inherent questions, had gone on for far too long. Would he be married with a family of his own? Would he be mean-spirited? Would he toss them out into the hedgerows with nary a second thought?

Were the lady to rely on Mr. Collins's letter alone, he surely satisfied her every notion of what Longbourn's heir ought to be. She was determined to be his staunchest supporter, knowing that she would remain in her home for the rest of her life once she had married off one of her girls to the new master.

"Mind your tongue, Child," cried Mrs. Bennet in response to her youngest's outburst. "In such a time as this, one can ill afford the luxury of marrying where one chooses. Why, if one of you girls were to marry Mr. Collins, then we will always have this house. None of us would ever risk destitution. I am sure that is what your father was thinking of when he passed away so unexpectedly that one of you would marry the heir to the estate. Why else would he have failed to break the entail before he died?"

Elizabeth almost wanted to roll her eyes. But what would have been the point? She had attempted on more than a few occasions since her father's passing to explain the rules of the entail to her mother but to little avail. Mrs. Bennet was just the sort of person who once having formed an opinion, however poorly conceived, stood by her original opinion to the end. Nothing anyone might say could make her change her mind. Her daughter had simply stopped trying.

Mrs. Bennet threw a glance about the room and examined her daughters one by one. She said, "Jane cannot marry Mr. Collins. Despite all her beauty, that gentleman will want a wife who can fully oversee his household. He will undoubtedly look right past her other amiable qualities and concentrate on what she cannot do rather than all that she can do."

As she was sitting next to her eldest daughter at the time, she placed her hand on Jane's. "Not that you have any reason to repine in that regard, my dear. No one blames you because you are blind. If anything, I blame that old horse you were riding at the time. What a beast!"

Jane merely offered her mother a smile, just as she always did when her mother went on in that way. Jane knew there really was no one to blame for the malady.

The tragic onset of her loss of sight had remained an unexplained calamity for more than a decade. The Bennet family's lack of fortune prohibited them from seeking a remedy beyond a perfunctory examination by a London physician. Restoring Jane's vision had been accepted as beyond anyone's power.

Jane had never seen Kitty and Lydia. Her memory of Mary (the third Bennet daughter) was primarily the product of a child's imagination. She was sure she would recognize her sister Elizabeth even among a crowd of young ladies were she once again blessed with a return of her sight. Until such time which may or may not come, Jane was largely beholden to her family to make sure she was cared for, and she could have no reason to suspect she might ever be any man's choice of a wife.

"No," Mrs. Bennet continued, "Mr. Collins is far

more likely to choose Lizzy to be his bride. She is, after all, second in age to Jane as well as in beauty. I posit you younger girls are quite safe."

Hearing this, Elizabeth's expression was beyond description. She, too, had spent a fair amount of time wondering what would happen when Longbourn's missing heir finally turned up. Her greatest fear was he would want nothing to do with the Bennets—that they would be forced to leave their home with little more than the clothes on their backs.

Her mother's inheritance was far too insignificant to provide for the six of them. No, her family would be torn apart, forced to rely on the generosity of family and friends if they were lucky but more likely forced to seek employment as governesses. The thought of her younger sisters, Kitty and Lydia, being governesses to anyone's children, was laughable and for a good reason. The two of them were scarcely more than children themselves, even if they were out in society.

She never once supposed that Longbourn's missing heir might be a single man in want of a wife. If Elizabeth had her way, neither she nor any of her sisters would marry Mr. Collins. She wanted nothing more than for him to go away and never come back. His so-called benevolence toward her family aside, the man was pompous and somewhat ridiculous.

Alas, the sad state of living in a home entailed away from the female line of the family took away every possibility for the Bennets to remain there in the absence of a marriage between a Bennet daughter and Longbourn's heir.

Elizabeth knew herself far too well to imagine that she would happily submit to such a scheme, even though her beloved father had relegated the care of her mother and sisters to her, upon his passing. That was but one of the reasons she held her tongue. The other reason was she had just escaped an ambush by none other than the gentleman himself in which he had attempted already to press his point.

Folding her hands in her lap, Elizabeth shifted in her chair a little. *Thankfully, I managed to put Mr. Collins off for now. I fear, however, I am only postponing the inevitable. I fear only a miracle will save me from my mother's prognostication.*

The younger girls' joy in hearing this was just as was what might be expected. "Thank heavens for that. Lizzy is so old anyway. She ought to be lucky to have Mr. Collins!"

Elizabeth, speaking up in her own defense, cried, "I am not that old!"

"Well," Lydia responded, shrugging, "You are on the

wrong side of twenty, which makes you plenty old to me."

"I could be Mr. Collins's choice," a quiet voice from the corner of the room could be heard saying.

Mrs. Bennet spun around in her seat. Every eye in the room trained on the third-born daughter. "What is that you just said, Mary?"

Mary cleared her throat and raised her voice. "I said I could very well be Mr. Collins's choice."

Her mother, as well as her two younger sisters, nearly laughed out loud.

"Mary!" the former exclaimed with energy. "How you enjoy speaking nonsense. Despite your habit of espousing Fordyce's Sermons to anyone who will listen, I highly doubt your doing so will be enough to garner the gentleman's favor, even if he does fancy himself a clergyman at heart. Mr. Collins seems far too proud and self-important not to set his cap on your sister Lizzy.

"Saying that," she continued, "I must applaud your optimism, however ill-founded it is. I am sure your heart is in the right place."

While Mrs. Bennet had been quick to dismiss Mary's opinion, at least one of the other occupants in the room most assuredly did not - specifically, Elizabeth.

# CHAPTER 5

*E*lizabeth's heart went out to her sister Mary, who, undoubtedly, did not like hearing such a rebuttal from her own mother. Mary, in consequence of being the only plain one in the family, was often the target of derision on account of it. She bore her lot with equanimity and always worked hard for knowledge and accomplishments. A striking contrast indeed to the younger sisters, Kitty and Lydia, who never took the time to accomplish much of anything that did not have to do with looking pretty, attending balls and assemblies, and flirting with gentlemen in scarlet coats.

Thus repulsed by her mother and sisters, Mary resumed reading her book. No doubt, upon fashioning a fitting retort to her mother's assertion, she would return to the debate.

Elizabeth could not help but think about Mary's assertion. If Mary was the one Bennet daughter who would gladly meet the ridiculous Mr. Collins at the marriage altar, why on earth would Elizabeth not do everything in her power to bring such an alliance about? The plain and simple fact was that the surest means of the Bennet ladies remaining at Longbourn was for one of them to marry Mr. Collins.

*As much as it pains me, I believe Mary's conjecture is the miracle I hoped for,* Elizabeth silently considered.

It was not as though she had accepted Mr. Collins's condescending proposal when he made it earlier that same day. She had simply asked for some time to think about it. And she had done it in such a way as not to extinguish any cause the man might have to hope. She had supposed she could postpone her decision long enough to find a means that would satisfy everyone's purpose and especially her own, and now, thanks to Mary, Elizabeth had cause to believe that she did indeed have the reason she had hoped for. As much as she loved her family and would do anything to see that they had every creature comfort they would need, a part of her was not entirely persuaded it would be in her best interest to sacrifice her own chance for felicity in the process.

Now thanks to her sister Mary, perhaps she would not have to. Thus decided, Elizabeth knew what she needed to do. She only needed to persuade Mr. William Collins to go along with her scheme.

---

Elizabeth found Mr. Collins in the library. What an odd fellow he was. Owing to his extraordinary deference to his noble patroness, Lady Catherine de Bourgh, Elizabeth was given to wonder if he was a sensible man or if he could be easily swayed. She would soon find out.

There he stood, staring out the window with his hands clutched behind his back. He was a tall, heavy-looking young man of five-and-twenty. His air was grave and stately, and his manners were very formal. His countenance was not entirely unpleasant, Elizabeth was forced to concede. She had undoubtedly seen far less attractive gentlemen in her time. Still, he was not half so appealing as she might have wished.

His current attitude was eerily reminiscent of her late father's. It bothered her more than a little, the proprietary nature with which he comported himself in her family's home as though thoroughly insensitive to the fact that to all of them, he was no more than a guest.

Were they to be faulted for suffering such human frailties? Yes, he was now the owner of the estate because of the entail away from the female line, but why laud it over all of them by comporting himself with such a lack of empathy or even sympathy.

Elizabeth, wanting to get the gentleman's attention, tapped on the door.

Mr. Collins turned. Grinning from ear to ear, the ridiculous man summoned Elizabeth inside the room.

"I knew you were far too kind to keep me in suspense for very long," he began. "Have you come to give me your decision? Although there can hardly be any doubt, I suppose a woman likes to think that her wishes hold sway. I fancy myself nothing at all if not considerate of the ladies." As though realizing how he must sound to a gently bred woman, he said, "Not that I shall ever give you cause to regret your decision, for faithfulness is akin to godliness. Once we are man and wife, I promise neither of us shall ever have cause to stray."

"Actually, sir," Elizabeth replied, "I appreciate the chance to consider your proposal with all the diligence that such a proposal warrants. In doing so, it dawned on me that such a weighty decision cannot possibly be made without the advice of one who is far more consequential than either of us. Thus, I came here to discuss a proposal of my own. That is if you will indulge me?"

"A proposal of your own? Do you mean a counter proposal?"

"If that is the way you choose to consider it, sir."

He nodded. "I am certainly open to hearing what you have to say."

"Sir, I want to make certain that," she said. "What I mean to say is I know how highly you esteem your noble patroness Lady Catherine de Bourgh's good opinion. No doubt, you would want her to look favorably on your match."

"If that is your concern, I can have no reason to believe Lady Catherine will not hold you in the highest esteem."

"But what if she does not? Despite being your own master, I am sure you would not wish to risk the loss of her highest approbation simply because of your choice of a wife. Would you not rather have her ladyship meet your future bride and give her blessings to a possible union before you commit to such an irrevocable decision?

"Did her ladyship not insinuate as much when you

two talked?" Elizabeth asked, harkening back to Mr. Collins's proposal to her in which he had elaborated in great detail his reason for doing so. She was sure she would never forget one particular part of his speech:

*"Upon the advice of the Right Honorable Lady Catherine de Bourgh, I am to choose wisely for her own sake, especially, should there be a possibility of any future connection between us. She further stipulated that I must choose judiciously for my own sake as well. The Bennet daughter of my choosing must be an active, useful sort of person and one who knows and understands a woman's place.*

*"Granted, the duration of our acquaintance is short, indeed. However, I can have no reason to suppose you, my fair cousin, will not suit my purposes perfectly well."*

Collins cupped his chin with his left hand and commenced tapping his index finger against his face. "Now that you mention it, I am certain Lady Catherine would appreciate such a gesture. She would be severely disappointed if she thought I chose poorly. But what do you propose? Surely you do not expect Lady Catherine de Bourgh to travel all the way to Hertfordshire."

"Heaven forbid the great lady should be expected

to do something as belittling as that. I posit you must write to the grand lady and prevail on her to invite the object of your affections to Kent. Were I you, I would further advise Lady Catherine that you have not, nor will you make your decision until you hear from her how you ought to act."

The gentleman smirked. "Are you suggesting the two of us enter into a secret engagement?"

Elizabeth shook her head. "Heavens, no! For what could be more scandalous and, dare I say, disrespectful toward the great lady? No, you and I must be totally above board. Lady Catherine must not only be persuaded that she is the final arbiter, but she must indeed be the final arbiter."

Mr. Collins rubbed his chin. At length, he said, "You have made a very compelling argument, Cousin Elizabeth. Indeed, I am almost ashamed of myself for not thinking of your proposal sooner. Of course, it only makes sense that the object of my affections and possibly my future bride must first be presented to Lady Catherine for her approval and her blessings. As for your being a guest in her home, I am sure it is the only arrangement that will suit, for as a man of God, which I am sure I will always be on some level, I am not so naïve as to suppose you might stay at the Parsonage.

"Now, the only thing that must be done is for me to write the necessary letter to Lady Catherine, prevailing on her to entertain the idea of allowing you to be a guest at Rosings Park. I can have no reason to suppose she will not be amenable to such a fine scheme as this, for she has more than enough room. You will be in nobody's way during your stay, I am sure."

"Wonderful!" Elizabeth said, covering her mouth with both hands to mask her triumphant smile. "I was hoping you would be agreeable to my proposal. That said, it is incumbent upon me to remind you that no mention of your earlier proposal is to cross either of our lips. And as for my being a guest at Rosings Park, it is of utmost importance to me that my sister Mary is also invited." To further bolster her stance, she added, "I do not believe that I would be comfortable being so far away from home without her. We are very close - as close as two sisters can be."

Elizabeth left the room feeling quite proud of herself. The scheme of hers was not without risks. *What if Mr. Collins is not able to persuade Lady Catherine de Bourgh to go along with the arrangement?*

The answer to the question, she dared not to contemplate.

*I shall not worry about the possibility of failure just yet.*

Her father's dying wish that she should take care of her family came to mind. Worry, she must. *Should my scheme to persuade Mr. Collins to set his cap on Mary fail, I shall have no other choice than to accept his hand in marriage.*

The very thought was enough to disrupt Elizabeth's equanimity. As she was not designed to dwell in misery, however, she soothed herself with another, more palatable option.

*The best case scenario would be for me to commit to a long drawn out engagement period, during which time Mr. Collins will meet with some mishap ... amnesia, for instance, a total loss of memory, and he will wander off to parts unknown and never be heard from again.*

# CHAPTER 6

*A*s a consequence of their journey, Elizabeth was well versed in almost everything there was to know about Lady Catherine de Bourgh as well as about her daughter Anne. If the gentleman was to be believed, the former was a saint and the latter was a goddess.

So eager was Mr. Collins to introduce her to his noble patroness that their trip from Hertfordshire to Kent did not afford the time to visit her relations in Cheapside, a Mr. and Mrs. Gardiner.

The gentleman's rationale had been that there would be time enough to visit the Gardiners after the engagement was in effect, but someone as consequential as Lady Catherine was not one to be kept waiting.

Thus, Elizabeth now found herself, along with her

sister Mary and the tedious Mr. Collins, standing directly before the grand lady in the parlor at Rosings.

"Dear cousins, allow me to present you to my noble patroness, Lady Catherine de Bourgh."

She was a fine figure of a woman, one who no doubt had known her fair share of beauty. She was wearing a silk gown that spoke of great wealth, and her neckline was draped by emeralds.

"So, you are the eldest daughter, Miss Bennet," the older woman said, her tone a mixture of curiosity and condescension. Peering over her spectacles, she eyed Elizabeth from head to toe as though expecting to find fault. If she meant to frighten Elizabeth by standing there in all her haughty air, she would have no such luck. The younger woman was not easily intimidated, preferring instead to laugh at pretension and ridiculousness.

"No, your ladyship," Elizabeth replied. "That distinction belongs to my sister Jane. I am the second eldest."

"Yes, begging your pardon, your ladyship. This is Miss Elizabeth Bennet," said Mr. Collins, his tone annoyingly contrite.

Lady Catherine asked, directing her eyes to Mary. "And who is this one?"

"This is Miss Mary Bennet," said Mr. Collins.

"And where do you fall in order of birth?"

"I am the third Bennet daughter, your ladyship," Mary replied somewhat timidly.

Now it was Mary's turn to be scrutinized from head to toe by Lady Catherine. The silent inspection completed, she said, "Well, well. Your sister is fairly tolerable, I suppose, but you are hardly anything to look at."

Elizabeth tried not to wince on her sister's behalf. *If this is the sort of hospitality we ought to expect, I fear it will be a long miserable stay in this part of the country.*

"You are both here as my guests, so I am obliged to do everything in my power to see to your comfort. I understand you traveled with only one servant. I suppose your mother could not spare any of the others. No doubt, your governess remains in Hertfordshire with your younger sisters. I was told there are two of them."

"Your ladyship is correct as regards the number of younger sisters," Elizabeth responded. "However, we never had a governess."

Lady Catherine stared aghast. By her expression, Elizabeth might as well have said they were penniless or worse, homeless, which the Bennets very well might be if her plan failed.

"No governess! How was that possible? Five

45

daughters brought up at home without a governess! I never heard of such a thing. Your mother must have been quite a slave to your education."

Elizabeth could hardly help smiling at Lady Catherine's indignation as she assured her that such had not been the case.

"Then, who taught you? Who attended to you? Without a governess, you must have been neglected."

"Compared with some families, I believe we were. But that is not to say that those of us who wished to learn never wanted the means. We were always encouraged to read and had all the necessary masters," Elizabeth explained.

Seizing the chance to promote Mary in the grand lady's esteem, Elizabeth continued. "Mary's musical acumen far exceeds that of all of us. She availed herself to the finest resources she could, and she practices most diligently."

"That speaks highly of your character, young woman," said Lady Catherine to Mary. "I shall be delighted to have you exhibit this evening. There are few people in England, I suppose, who have more enjoyment of music than myself, or a better natural taste. If I had ever learned, I should have been a great proficient. And so, as well, would Anne, if her health had allowed her to apply.

"The two of you shall have the pleasure of meeting my Anne later. For now, she is resting." She looked at Elizabeth. "By the looks of you and your sister, you could also do with a rest before coming down for dinner." Her eyes sought out the closest servant. "Please see the Bennet ladies to their rooms."

---

Once Elizabeth and Mary quit the room, Mr. Collins, too, prepared to take his leave.

"I would have a word with you before you go, Mr. Collins."

He immediately resumed his former attitude.

Lady Catherine began, "Were one to judge by appearances alone, Mr. Collins, one might say you have chosen wisely, but only time will tell. There is something to admire in the eldest Bennet daughter, I suppose.

"As I understand, based on your letter, nothing is set in stone, and to that, I say it is just as well. You were wise indeed to seek my counsel before anything is decided." She scoffed and flipped open her fan. "No governess, indeed."

Fanning herself, she appeared to be in deep

contemplation. Collins shifted a little in his chair, drawing her attention.

"That will be all," she said, setting aside her fan. He stood, bowed, and headed toward the door only to be stopped by the sound of her ladyship's voice.

"I should expect you to join us for dinner this evening."

"It is my honor."

"Very well. Prepare yourself to be quite diverted, for there are to be additions to our party. My nephews are visiting Rosings Park as well."

---

Once Elizabeth was alone, she collapsed on her bed. After spending less than a quarter of an hour with Lady Catherine, she was entirely persuaded that she had just met one of the most opinionated, most officious people in the world. She sighed. *If this is what staying at Rosings Park entails, it is going to be quite a challenge.*

Her apartment was everything a room in such a manor house ought to be, even if it was a bit too ostentatious for Elizabeth's liking. Mary was settling in just across the hallway.

Shutting her eyes, Elizabeth tried willing herself to

sleep. But sleep would not come. How could it when most of the trip to Kent had been spent either sleeping or pretending to sleep in order to avoid conversing with Mr. Collins? The advantage of such a stratagem was that time had allowed ample opportunity for Mary to engage with the gentleman.

The two of them had had so much in common–all the makings of felicity in marriage so far as Elizabeth was concerned.

*Indeed, it seems my plan is working.*

And just in case her scheme did not bear fruit, no one would know, for Elizabeth had not confided in anyone her intention to unite Mary and Mr. Collins. How unfair it would be for Mary if she knew. Even if she believed Mary would willingly go along with such a scheme, Elizabeth did not mean to risk injuring her sister whose expectations might be raised only to be disappointed.

After a half-hour in that same restless attitude, Elizabeth arose from the bed and drifted toward the window. Not only was she restless, but she was teeming with curiosity. Curiosity about the manor house, its inhabitants, and mostly the park itself.

She determined to get away, if only for an hour or so. She had admired the beauty of Rosings Park, and she did not wish to wait until the next day to begin exploring its many lanes. She made her way out of doors without being detected, and she walked and walked and admired everything she saw.

Before she knew what she was about, a village loomed just up ahead. Thus compelled, she walked on. Soon enough, she came upon a shop, and she peered inside the window. It was a quaint little establishment much like the shops in Meryton, the small town near her home in Hertfordshire.

Elizabeth decided to go inside, hoping that she might find one of the books that had long topped her list of desired reading materials which she had been unable to procure in Meryton.

*What is the harm in checking to see if it is available in this particular shop?*

Elizabeth recognized that the odds of the shop-keeper having the book were minuscule, but she would not forgive herself if she did not at least ask. She risked nothing in doing so and thus made her way to the counter.

The shopkeeper welcomed her with a broad smile. "How may I be of service to you, madam?"

"Sir, I am hoping that you are in possession of the book, *St. Irvyne*. It was recently published, albeit anonymously as 'by a Gentleman of the University of Oxford', I believe."

He frowned. "I am sorry to disappoint you; however, I do not have that particular book in stock at this time. I will be happy to order it for you."

"Oh, no! That will not be necessary. You see, I am merely visiting this part of the country, and I do not plan to remain very long. I thank you for your consideration." With that, Elizabeth decided she would peruse some other merchandise on display available in the shop.

*Surely there must be something here of interest to me.*

Moments later, a tall, handsome gentleman entered the establishment and proceeded directly to the counter. The shopkeeper, upon seeing the gentleman, stopped everything that he was doing and rushed to the counter.

"Mr. Darcy, how delighted I am by your presence. Indeed, I was hoping that you would patronize my humble establishment during your visit. Indeed, I have the first edition of *St. Irvyne* which I suspected might be of some interest to you. I went so far as to set it aside expressly for you."

"Indeed, that is precisely the reason for my visit this afternoon. You are a good man. Thank you for anticipating my needs yet again. I can think of no better companion during my visit."

"Capital," said the shopkeeper. "If you will pardon me, I shall retrieve it directly."

"Take your time," said the tall gentleman, removing his leather gloves. "I am in no particular rush this afternoon."

As she was standing nearby the counter, Elizabeth could not help but hear the entire exchange between the shopkeeper and the other gentleman. Suffice it to say, she was not pleased. No one liked being lied to, and she was persuaded that is precisely what the shopkeeper had done. He lied to her about not having the book in stock and added insult to injury by offering to order a copy for her.

Seeing that the tall gentleman had stepped away from the counter, Elizabeth seized the chance to question the shopkeeper and call him out for his duplicity.

She approached the counter and cleared her throat, hoping to capture the merchant's attention. But to no avail. She cleared her throat again and still was unable to summon his attention. Elizabeth had hoped to avoid drawing attention to herself, but as her attempts to be discreet had proven futile, she rang the bell on the countertop. Elizabeth had not expected it to resound throughout the establishment as loudly as it did. Now, she had everyone's attention.

"May I help you?" The shopkeeper inquired upon turning around to face Elizabeth.

"Yes, you may, sir. You might begin by clearing up a bit of confusion on my part."

"Pardon?"

"Indeed, when I inquired about the book, *St. Irvyne*, I am certain you said you did not have a single copy in the store and yet, you were all too eager to produce a copy for that gentleman over there."

"Well–about that. you see Miss –?"

"Miss Bennet," Elizabeth replied.

"Yes, well, Miss Bennet, the gentleman to whom you are referring is not just anyone. He is Mr. Fitzwilliam Darcy. He is a most loyal customer."

"Be that as it may, you could have no way of knowing he would frequent your lovely establishment today or if he would even desire the book that I inquired about. Rather than sell it on a first-come, first-served basis, you opted to hold it back, just in case. Is the value of my money less than the value of that gentleman's?"

The shopkeeper hardly knew how to look or how to feel in the wake of Elizabeth's rebuke. However, as Mr. Darcy's attention was also drawn, he suffered no such affliction.

"Is there a problem here?" he asked, having

approached Elizabeth and the shopkeeper at the counter. First, he looked at the shopkeeper, and then he looked at Elizabeth.

What a commanding presence this stranger was, now standing directly beside Elizabeth. If he meant to intimidate her, he had gotten off to a good start.

*Mr. Fitzwilliam Darcy. Mr. Fitzwilliam Darcy,* Elizabeth silently repeated, suffering the weight of his stare. His dark, brooding eyes seem to pore all over her, and she began to think she might grow afraid of him if she did not say something.

"Either there is a problem or a deliberate misunderstanding between the shopkeeper and me. For the sake of civility, I would rather prefer the latter."

"Yes, yes," the older man began, "a misunderstanding is precisely what it is. You see, Mr. Darcy, the young lady–"

"Miss Bennet," Darcy interrupted, his dark eyes fixed on her.

The sound of her name uttered by the tall, handsome stranger nearly took Elizabeth's breath away. How familiar he sounded, indeed intimate.

*Perhaps he will relinquish the book to me once he hears the entire account of what unfolded before he entered the establishment. It is only fair.*

"Yes, Miss Bennet," the other man said, nodding his

head, "happened to ask about the book moments before you entered the shop."

"I did, indeed," Elizabeth added. "Only to be told by the shopkeeper that he did not have a single copy of the book in stock, when in fact he was holding it back on the chance that you might come along and claim it for yourself, Mr.–" here Elizabeth paused, feigning ignorance as regarded the gentleman's surname. Never mind that she had committed not only his name, but everything else about his handsome person to memory.

"Allow me to introduce myself. I am Fitzwilliam Darcy," he said bowing. He took Elizabeth's gloved hand into his and brushed a kiss atop her knuckles. Releasing her hand, he resumed his former attitude. His eyes met hers. "It is a pleasure to make your acquaintance."

Ignoring the fluttering in her stomach, Elizabeth replied, "I know the proper thing to say is the pleasure is all mine, but surely given the circumstances, you will pardon me if I cannot."

"Circumstances, Miss Bennet?"

"Surely you will concede to the injustice of what has unfolded, Mr. Darcy."

The shopkeeper interrupted them. "If the two of you will pardon me, I need to retrieve the book from the back." He was gone directly.

Mr. Darcy clasped his hands behind his back. The manner in which he regarded her from head to toe gave her to wonder if he was looking at her merely to find fault.

"So, you contend it is unfair for a merchant to anticipate the needs of a most loyal patron at someone else's expense?"

*Who is this man?*

"Well—when you put it that way," she retorted, half annoyed by the condescending nature of this question, half derisive. "How is it not unfair?" Elizabeth continued. "How difficult would it have been for him to say I only have one copy in stock, and it is being reserved?"

Mr. Darcy arched his brow. "Somehow, I doubt you would have been pleased with such a response."

"Sir, you know nothing about me."

"I believe you like to have your own way; else you would have said nothing at all to the shopkeeper about how he chooses to conduct his business."

Now it was Elizabeth's turn to arch her brow. "And I believe you are far too opinionated and officious, else you would have stayed on the other side of the room and not cast yourself in the middle of my discussion with another."

"So, you are headstrong and unhindered, and I am

opinionated and officious. What a pair the two of us make."

She scoffed. "We are hardly a pair, Mr. Darcy. Indeed, we are total strangers."

The shopkeeper returned with a nicely wrapped parcel in his hand. "Will you be paying for this in the usual way, Mr. Darcy?" he asked, poised to hand it over.

Darcy nodded. "Yes, my account. Pray, leave it there for now if you would," he said, gesturing to the countertop.

"But, of course," uttered the shopkeeper. He placed the package on the counter and walked away, once again leaving Darcy and Elizabeth to themselves.

"Total strangers, indeed," Mr. Darcy uttered. "However, we may not necessarily remain that way." He picked up the book. "I want you to have this."

"No, sir! I could not accept such a gift."

"Why not? It is clear that this book means more to you than it does to me. Please accept it. Consider it as less of a gift, but an olive branch, if you will. It is my way of making amends for any unpleasantness you had to endure."

Elizabeth was not about to argue the point all afternoon. She really did want to read that particular book during her stay in Kent, so accept it, she did.

"Thank you, sir," she said. "Perhaps our paths will cross again, at which point I might reciprocate your kindness. Indeed, I may even return your kindness in the form of this very book."

The smile that spread across his face in hearing this nearly took Elizabeth's breath away.

"In a village the size of this, no doubt our paths shall cross again. That being said, perhaps you will allow me to see you home safely. I imagine you are here visiting acquaintances."

A sense of panic rose up in Elizabeth. She could well imagine Lady Catherine would be livid were she to return to Rosings with a complete stranger. Making matters worse, she had escaped the manor house without telling the grand lady of her plans.

"No!" Elizabeth said. Remembering herself, she added, "What I meant to say is, I am in no need of an escort, sir. The rest of my party is close by. I fear I have kept them waiting long enough." Elizabeth did not like to speak untruthfully. She reasoned that Rosings Park really was close by, under three miles, and as for keeping her party waiting, if she did not make haste, they would indeed be waiting.

*No harm, no foul,* she told herself.

Clutching her gift to her bosom, Elizabeth smiled a little. "Thank you again, Mr. Darcy." With a slight curtsy, she quickly went on her way. She paused only after placing her hand on the door handle. Perched to open the door, she glanced back and was more than a little pleased to find the gentleman still looking at her.

The same gentleman whose brooding dark eyes had held her captivated, whom she had described as opinionated and officious, and who had gifted her a costly new book, was still looking at her.

*Perhaps our paths will cross again.*

For Elizabeth's part, she hoped it would be much sooner rather than later.

# CHAPTER 7

*M iss Bennet.*

Darcy smiled in the recollection of his earlier encounter with the young lady. He never thought of himself as someone who was easily distracted by a pair of fine eyes, but there he was reliving every second of his time spent with her.

*I wonder if I will ever see her again.*

In all of his years visiting that part of the country, Darcy could honestly say he had never come across a more intriguing creature than Miss Bennet.

*Miss Bennet.*

Before entering the shop that afternoon, Darcy had been riddled with concern over his inability to be in two places at one time. His friend, Charles Bingley, had been more than a little disappointed that Darcy's arrival in Hertfordshire would be delayed. However, his own family business required the latter to be in Kent. Such dissonance had all but dissipated. For now, his mind was full of but one thing or rather one person: the mysterious stranger in the shop.

He found himself repeating her name out loud as he rode along on horseback to Rosings Park. As he was in no particular hurry to return to the manor house, he encouraged his stallion to trod along at a snail's pace.

*Miss Bennet.*

Darcy exhaled. *Why do I feel I have heard her name before?*

*Could it be that I heard the mention of Miss Bennet's name from Lady Catherine?* He pursed his lips. *Her ladyship is always going on and on about the business of the parish and the like, so much so that I rarely attend a word she says.*

He started searching his memory for those bits and pieces he could recall of his aunt's most recent ramblings.

*I do recall some mentioning of guests.*

The citing of her vicar's name as a precursor to his aunt's speech had rendered the entire discourse mute to Darcy's ears. A more thorough racking of his brain, however, soon confirmed that which he had by now taught himself to hope. Spurring his stallion on, Darcy could hardly wait to reach the manor house.

Elizabeth's worst suspicions about Mr. Collins's deficits in terms of sensibility were confirmed when she was introduced to Lady Catherine's daughter, Miss Anne de Bourgh. She recalled in vivid detail the way he had described the young heiress. How eloquent the gentleman had been in her praise:

*"She is a most charming young lady, indeed. Lady Catherine herself says that, in point of true beauty, Miss de Bourgh is far superior to the handsomest of her sex because there is that in her features which marks the young lady of distinguished birth."*

In Mr. Collins's defense, he had mentioned Miss de Bourgh's being of a sickly constitution.

*What an understatement,* Elizabeth silently surmised. She was astonished at Miss de Bourgh's being so thin and so small. There was neither in figure nor face any likeness between the young woman and her aristocratic mother. Miss de Bourgh's features, though not plain, were insignificant, and she spoke in a low voice, which Elizabeth could scarcely hear. *What a striking contrast to Lady Catherine, indeed.*

Mary, if she did share a similar opinion as Elizabeth's of Miss de Bourgh, did not betray any signs. Instead, she took the seat next to the young heiress. Another woman, a Mrs. Jenkinson, had been introduced as Miss de Bourgh's companion.

There the ladies sat and listened as Lady Catherine prognosticated on what the weather would be during the course of the week and pontificated on how her guests ought to plan on spending their time during their stay in Kent.

Elizabeth barely attended a word being said. Her mind was busily engaged in thinking of the encounter with the tall, handsome stranger at the shop. Even now, her heart skipped a beat just thinking about him. She had gone from being intrigued by him, to being perturbed by him, to being fascinated by him in the span of a quarter-hour.

*Mr. Fitzwilliam Darcy.*

An odd feeling came over her. She had not allowed herself to indulge in such flights of fancy in more than a year—not since her beloved father had passed away. Overnight, it seemed, she had gone from being a carefree maiden whose marital prospects, though limited by the size of her family's fortune, were something to be viewed with hope, to the de facto head of the family, responsible for securing her family's future.

Even such weighty burdens as these would not diminish the excitement she felt in having met Mr. Darcy.

*I really do hope our paths soon cross again.*

All heads turned when the object of Elizabeth's musings entered the room.

"Mr. Darcy!" she exclaimed, forgetting herself.

Taken aback, Lady Catherine said, "Do you know my nephew?"

"Your nephew?" Elizabeth's heart nearly sank in her chest. *What if he is just like his aunt?*

Mr. Darcy said, "I had the great pleasure of meeting Miss Bennet earlier today, Lady Catherine."

"Earlier today? How can that be when the young woman only arrived a few hours ago? Where exactly did this meeting take place?"

"We met at a shop on Meeting Street," Elizabeth confessed.

"Meeting Street? How is that possible when you were meant to go to your room and rest? How could you possibly have been in two places at one time?"

"I wasn't tired, your ladyship, and after traveling for so long in the carriage, I was in need of exercise, and so I decided to take a walk about your lovely grounds. Before I knew what I was about, I was in the village."

"Why! The village is over three miles away!"

Elizabeth nodded. "I am very fond of walking."

"I never heard of such a thing. A young lady traipsing about the countryside." Lady Catherine scoffed. "Fond of walking indeed." She threw a glance at Mary. "Does that mean you, too, have a habit of exhibiting such recklessness?"

"No, your ladyship," Mary replied. "My sister is known as the great walker in our family. I can hardly keep up. I much prefer remaining indoors."

The older woman nodded her approval. "That is precisely what I expected you to say. You strike me as being a sensible young lady and one who knows a woman's place."

Mr. Collins's words immediately came to Elizabeth's mind: *"The Bennet daughter of my choosing must be an active, useful sort of person and one who knows and understands a woman's place."*

*From Lady Catherine's mouth to Mr. Collins's ears,* Elizabeth silently prayed. *This bodes well for my sister, indeed.*

Before she could dwell too long on her sister's prospects, another gentleman entered the room.

What a relief it was when Lady Catherine focused her attention on the newcomer. "There you are, Fitzwilliam," she said. She could not have missed the interested manner in which he regarded Elizabeth. "Pray, tell me that you are not acquainted with my guest as well."

"I should be so fortunate," he said, approaching Elizabeth directly. "Colonel Fitzwilliam at your service," he said with a slight bow. Taking Elizabeth's hand in his, he bestowed a light kiss upon it before resuming his former attitude.

Elizabeth felt the color spread all over her body. It did not go unnoticed by her that Mr. Darcy appeared to take umbrage with the gentleman's behavior.

Lady Catherine said, "That will be quite enough of that, Fitzwilliam." She gestured for him to move away from Elizabeth, which he did, taking his place standing beside Mr. Darcy. Their aunt continued, "I take it that neither of you has met the other Miss Bennet in the room. This is Miss Mary Bennet."

Both men greeted Mary with bows, the colonel's far more gracious than Mr. Darcy's.

"You two will recall my telling you that Mr. Collins, the vicar, traveled to his recently inherited estate to meet his relations. The Bennet daughters are but two of them. If things go as planned, well, let me just say that family's misfortunes are soon to be elevated."

"That sounds rather intriguing. Dare I ask you to elaborate?" Colonel Fitzwilliam inquired.

"You would be wise to mind your own business, Nephew."

Next, her ladyship's butler walked into the room. "Mr. William Collins," he announced.

Elizabeth, as much as she wanted to resume where she and Mr. Darcy had left off at the shop, had but one purpose in mind for the evening. That being to elevate her sister Mary in Mr. Collins's esteem.

*There will be time enough to get better acquainted with Mr. Darcy, as well as with Colonel Fitzwilliam, who, incidentally, has not taken his eyes off me.*

# CHAPTER 8

The dinner was exceedingly handsome, and there were all the servants and all the articles of plate which one might expect of a hostess as noble as Lady Catherine de Bourgh. She was exceedingly impressed with herself as evidenced by her noble manner and her speech. "I do not suppose I have to tell you, young ladies, how fortunate you are to be dining among such lofty company this evening. I rightly suppose you have had no such opportunities in Hertfordshire. In a country neighborhood, you move in a very confined and unvarying society."

"On the contrary, your ladyship. Our society is rather more diverse than one would expect. That is not to say it is so vast as in town, but I suppose there are few neighborhoods larger. I know we dine with four-and-twenty families."

"I suppose I do recall a gentleman who hailed from Hertfordshire, who was an acquaintance of my late husband, Sir Louis de Bourgh. If I remember correctly, his name is Coble. The last I heard, he was recently widowed—his third wife, I believe. I do not suppose your families are acquainted."

Elizabeth shuddered at the notion. The two families were by no means close, but she had undoubtedly heard of the gentleman and his plight. With three wives dead, he was practically a legend. And not in a good way. He was whispered to be the *'merry'* widower. With each new wife came an increase in his fortune.

*The less spoken about that particular gentleman, the better*, Elizabeth thought.

Lady Catherine continued, "Aside from Mr. Coble, I grant you none of the other families you mentioned are of any real consequence."

Not willing to be dismissed and not seeking to be contrite, Elizabeth grasped for the most persuasive argument she could find. "Sir William Lucas, whose estate abuts Longbourn, would beg to differ." What did it matter to her that 'estate' was hardly an apt characterization of the gentleman's home, which he had dubbed Lucas Lodge? *What are the chances Lady Catherine will ever be in a position to refute my assertion?*

"Upon my word," said her ladyship, "you give your opinion very decidedly for so young a person. Pray, what is your age?"

"With three younger sisters grown up," replied Elizabeth, smiling, "your ladyship can hardly expect me to own it."

Elizabeth's response must have mortified Mr. Collins. "Pray, Cousin Elizabeth, her ladyship's question deserves a more fitting response, does it not?"

"You cannot be more than twenty, I am sure; therefore, you need not conceal your age," her ladyship added.

"I am not one-and-twenty."

"How difficult was that to admit?" Lady Catherine asked. "I suppose it is the fashion to be unnecessarily contrary merely for the sake of it." She threw a glance at Mary. "Although I do not suppose you would employ such stratagems, young lady."

Mary retrieved her linen napkin, ostensibly, to brush it across her lips. Elizabeth knew what her sister was really about. No doubt, Mary was searching her memory for an antidote - one from Fordyce's sermons - to support her response.

Clearing her throat, Mary said, "I am ever mindful

of the danger that lest young women should lose in softness what they gained in force. The pursuit of such elevation should interfere as little as possible with the plain duties and humble virtues of life."

"You see, Miss Bennet, that is precisely how a young lady ought to feel."

Elizabeth wanted to roll her eyes, not at her sister, for Mary would not be Mary if she were not espousing Fordyce's, however convoluted her analogies. But Elizabeth was sure that Lady Catherine had never once given herself the trouble of reading Fordyce's sermons.

*I would sooner expect her ladyship to claim she had written them or, at the very least, she would have written them if she had had the chance.*

What a relief that a brief lull in the conversation was soon interrupted by Lady Catherine's focusing her attention on her nephews.

"How does Georgiana get on, Darcy?"

"My sister is getting on very well," Mr. Darcy replied, darting his eyes toward Elizabeth as if speaking for her benefit.

"I hope she is not neglecting her playing."

"No, she is not."

"I am delighted to hear such a good account of her," said Lady Catherine. "Pray, tell her from me that she cannot expect to excel if she does not practice a good deal."

"I assure you, madam," he replied, "that she does not need such advice. She practices very constantly."

"So much the better. It cannot be done too much. When I next write to her, I shall charge her not to neglect it on any account. I often tell young ladies that no excellence in music is to be acquired without constant practice.

"I have been told Miss Mary already adheres to this advice. I am sure we shall all be delighted to have you exhibit for us after dinner, young woman."

Mary nodded her acquiescence to her ladyship's scheme. As her sister was always eager for such chances to demonstrate her prowess, Elizabeth was sure Mary would exhibit on the pianoforte every waking moment if she thought she could get away with it.

"And what of yourself?" the colonel inquired, speaking to Elizabeth.

Elizabeth would have given the gentleman a look that shot daggers if they had been better acquainted, for this was not a conversation she wanted to be drawn into. As they were mere hours into their acquaintance, she did not do so, however. Elizabeth discerned the colonel to be an amiable man who fell quickly into conversation wherever he went. She supposed she would have time to be entirely at ease with him soon enough.

Her mind wandered to earlier that afternoon when she first made Mr. Darcy's acquaintance. She had most certainly not exercised such caution with him. The reason she felt so reserved with one gentleman and so uninhibited with the other was something she was looking forward to finding out.

"It seems Miss Bennet's musical acumen is not on par with her sister's," Lady Catherine replied in the wake of Elizabeth's silence.

"And why is that?" Mr. Darcy asked.

"I fear I have no one to blame but myself, Mr. Darcy," she replied. "You see, sir, I never take time to practice."

When he could, Mr. Collins approached Elizabeth in the hallway leading to the drawing-room after dinner.

"Cousin Elizabeth," he began in earnest, "if I may, pray, allow me to caution you on your behavior toward Lady Catherine. One who would ever dare to trifle with so much dignified impertinence is not likely one who would garner her ladyship's good opinion. Need I remind you of the reason for your being here?"

Without awaiting Elizabeth's response, Mr. Collins

turned on his heel and went away. It was good riddance so far as Elizabeth was concerned. The last thing the gentleman needed to hear, and indeed, the last thing she needed to say was what was really on her mind.

*I must think of my sister Mary*, Elizabeth reminded herself as she entered the drawing-room. *I must think of Mary.*

# CHAPTER 9

*D*ay after day passed, and yet Mr. Darcy and Colonel Fitzwilliam had not taken their leave from Kent even though Lady Catherine had repeatedly lamented that they would. The gentlemen's continued presence in that part of the country was a boon for Elizabeth. She liked them very much, and even though they were residing under the same roof, rarely did they have a chance to get better acquainted with each other. Not under Lady Catherine's watchful eyes.

Elizabeth's frequent walks about the park not only afforded her much-needed escapes from her ladyship's company, but they also afforded the company of one or the other of the lady's nephews, who often joined her.

On that particular day, she encountered Mr. Darcy. He seemed an entirely different man when outside his haughty aunt's presence. When in her ladyship's company, he was taciturn, rarely giving himself the trouble to speak unless called upon directly to do so. When walking about the grounds with Elizabeth, he talked with abandon. His speech was both elegant and purposeful, even though what his purposes might be, Elizabeth could not always discern.

Mr. Darcy was clever – a man of sense and education. She liked that about him. Few men of his acquaintance exhibited such admirable traits.

*I posit Mr. Darcy is very much like my father in that regard.*

Mr. Bennet, when he was alive, was so odd a mixture of quick parts, sarcastic humor, reserve, and caprice. Few understood and appreciated him as much as Elizabeth did—an admiration on her part that had been the means of their special bond.

Though she and Mr. Darcy were barely acquainted, she suspected he and her father would have had many things in common. The most significant exception being capriciousness, she supposed.

*Mr. Darcy is far too serious for one to mistake him as being impulsive or fanciful.*

However, conversations with the gentleman were

the closest thing to talking with her father – something she had been missing even more than she knew.

The topic of her family's situation evidently weighing on his own mind, Mr. Darcy said, "Pray, forgive me if what I am about to ask sounds unfeeling, but you must tell me how securing your family's future is your responsibility?"

For a second, Elizabeth was taken aback by his inquiry, wondering what its impetus had been. Then she recalled having spoken of her responsibilities at Longbourn in the wake of Mr. Bennet's passing. She had no idea that Mr. Darcy had been listening so intently.

"Is securing your own family's future not your responsibility, sir?"

"Of course, it is, but our situations are not comparable."

"Oh! And why is that? And do not tell me it is because you are the heir of a vast estate and its master, whereas I am a lowly female whose family's estate is entailed to the male line of the family, specifically a stranger who appeared at Longhorn's doorstep out of nowhere."

"The differences in our situation have less to do with gender and everything to do with connections and fortune. It is not my wish to argue with you but to merely point out the obvious. Besides that, you are much too young to be tasked with such a heavy burden."

"Well, such just happens to be my fate—a consequence of my being my late father's favorite daughter. Besides, someone had to step into my father's shoes. Who better than his favorite daughter, or in his own words the son he never had?"

"Forgive me if I am speaking out of line, however, do I correctly understand you to say you are effectively the head of the family?"

Elizabeth nodded. "For all intents and purposes, that is correct, sir. Does this come as a surprise to you? It is not unheard of that a woman should find herself in such a position, I am sure."

"What of your mother? Or perhaps your older sister? If I recall correctly, you are the second eldest daughter."

"Well, sir, to know my mother is to know precisely why not her. And as far as my older sister is concerned, I know that were she in the position to do so, she would gladly shoulder what you perceive is my burden. Fate, however, had other plans for my sister Jane."

"Fate? Do you care to elaborate?"

"I would rather not if you do not mind. Perhaps it

is a subject that we might discuss once we are better acquainted with each other."

"Fair enough. As for your father, I take it that you and he were very close."

"Indeed. We were as close as a father and daughter could wish to be. He was the best man in the world. I do not mean to say Papa was not without fault, however. I am sure no one could boast of such a trait. Aside from Lady Catherine," she added in jest. "However, apart from my older sister, Jane, my father was everything to me."

Elizabeth could not imagine why she was saying all these things to Mr. Darcy – aspects of her personal affairs she had never spoken about to anyone, not even Jane.

*I suppose there is something about confiding in a stranger that makes it so much easier to expose one's innermost thoughts.*

If Elizabeth thought it was something more than Mr. Darcy's merely being a stranger, she was not in a position of admitting it to herself. She had only known this man for a short duration, and yet she felt as though she had known him all her life.

On another day, Elizabeth was engaged as she walked, perusing her friend Charlotte's latest letter. If only she could have received such an intelligible correspondence from one of her own family. Alas, it was not to be. Mrs. Bennet's primary concern was Elizabeth's possible courtship with the heir of Longbourn. How disappointed she was that Elizabeth was determined to keep them all in suspense. That Elizabeth might receive another such offer of marriage was impossible for the lady to conceive. Therefore, Elizabeth had much better get Mr. Collins to the wedding altar before he died, and the search for the next heir ensued once again. Such was Mrs. Bennet's thinking.

Mrs. Bennet was as excited about the pending arrival of the Netherfield party as Elizabeth suspected her to be, but the former could only imagine Kitty or Lydia as a prospect for such an advantageous alliance. She did allow in her writing that Jane, too, might have been a viable candidate, were it not for her particular affliction.

*Thank heavens for dear Charlotte,* Elizabeth considered. Her younger sisters were certainly of no use, for they never took the time to write.

Charlotte had also made mention of the recent arrival of the militia in Hertfordshire. Indeed, they were camped just outside of Meryton. Closing her eyes, Elizabeth imagined all the glories of the camp - its tents stretched forth in beauteous uniformity of lines, crowded with the young and the gay, and dazzling with scarlet. To complete the view, she saw her youngest sister, Lydia, seated beneath a tent, tenderly flirting with at least six officers at once.

Opening her eyes, Elizabeth shook her head to ward off such thoughts. *My consolation is that Lydia is luckily too poor to be an object of prey to anybody. At most, she will be perceived as little more than a common flirt. The officers will find women better worth their notice.*

Still, a part of her could not help but be a little concerned. She was dwelling on those passages regarding the militia's presence, when, instead of being again surprised by Mr. Darcy, she saw on looking up that Colonel Fitzwilliam was meeting her. Putting away the letter immediately and forcing a smile, she said,

"This is a pleasant surprise seeing you, sir."

"I assure you the pleasure is all mine. Are you going much farther?"

"No, I should have turned in a moment."

And accordingly, she did turn, and they walked towards the manor house together.

"Do you intend to remain here in Kent much longer?" she asked.

"That I cannot say. It is entirely up to my cousin. As a point of fact, we should have taken our leave a while ago; however, the days continue to roll by with no sign of my cousin wishing to depart. This is quite uncharacteristic of him if I must say so myself, for he usually does not remain here in Kent very long once Lady Catherine's business concerns are settled. This time seems to be different. I can only surmise his reasoning has to do with you."

"Me?"

"What else can it be? Not that I fault him one bit. Your lovely presence has added an element to Rosings Park that has been genuinely missing for a long, long time."

"As flattered as I am by your generous speech, I find it hard to fathom. Indecisive is not exactly how I would describe your cousin."

"Oh? How exactly would you describe him?"

A thousand ways to describe Mr. Darcy immediately came to Elizabeth's mind – an alluring mixture of reserve and intrigue, dark and brooding, at times, yet charming and engaging at others.

*How might I begin to describe Mr. Darcy to another when I have not quite figured him out for myself?*

"Sir, surely you are in a better position than I am to describe your cousin."

"Fair enough," the colonel said. "Darcy is by far, one of the best men I know. He is an excellent master, a loving and protective brother, and a most loyal friend. There is nothing he would not do for those whom he considers most important to him."

"A man without fault?"

"He has his fair share of faults. Who among us does not? In my cousin's case, he likes to have his own way very well," replied Colonel Fitzwilliam. "But, then again, so we all do. It is only that he has better means of having it than many others, because he is rich, and many others are poor. I speak feelingly. A younger son, you know, must be inured to self-denial and dependence."

"In my opinion, the younger son of an earl can know very little of either. Now seriously, what have you ever known of self-denial and dependence? When has want of money prevented you from going wherever you chose or procuring anything you had a fancy for?"

"These are sound questions, and perhaps I cannot say that I have experienced many hardships of that nature. But in matters of greater weight, I may suffer from want of money. Younger sons cannot marry where they like."

"Unless where they like women of fortune, which I think they very often do."

"Our habits of expense make us too dependent. There are too many in my rank of life who can afford to marry without some attention to money."

*Is his speech meant for me?*

Elizabeth was more than a little bothered that he may have meant it as such. She hoped she did not show it.

"And pray, what is the usual price of an earl's younger son?" she said in a lively tone. "Unless the elder brother is very sickly, I suppose you would not ask above fifty thousand pounds."

He answered her in the same style, and the subject dropped. To interrupt a silence which might make him fancy her affected with what had passed, she soon afterward said, "In all sincerity, bearing such self-serving marital burdens is not solely the purview of a second son, sir."

"Why do I suppose we are no longer speaking hypothetically, Miss Bennet?"

*Because we are not,* Elizabeth thought but did not say. Perhaps if she were speaking with Mr. Darcy, she would have attempted to fashion a fitting response. However, Elizabeth was nowhere near as forthcoming with the colonel as she was with his cousin. She preferred to keep it that way.

The view of the manor house looming ahead put an end to the discussion as well as the walk, but it hardly settled her busy mind. The colonel had never been an object for her for anything other than amicable conversation. This knowing raised the question, the answer to which she did not know.

*When exactly did I come to expect something more meaningful with Mr. Darcy?*

# CHAPTER 10

*P*erhaps if Elizabeth had been paying more attention to where she was going, as opposed to having her head buried in her book, she would not have taken a wrong turn, and she assuredly would not found herself in her current predicament.

And what a predicament in which to find herself.

She gulped, thus catching Mr. Darcy off guard - standing there in his own room - stepping out of his bath with a towel in both hands, drying his hair.

Part of Elizabeth knew exactly what she must do. Turn away, of course, begging the gentlemen's pardon for the unintentional intrusion.

But, did one turn away when first espying a marble statue of Hercules? Did one turn away when beholding a statue of Zeus? Or any of the many other ancient marble statues? Mr. Darcy, in all his glory, was as close to a magnificent work of art as Elizabeth had ever beheld. A living breathing Adonis.

Though he stood there, as if frozen in time, his telling response amid her silent inspection spoke volumes.

*Turn away*, she silently beckoned in vain.

*Back away*, her silent thoughts beckoned instead. A command which Elizabeth heeded. First, a step. Then two, and finally, she dropped her book, she turned, and she hurried away.

Moments later, she found herself out of doors. Elizabeth's self-reproach would not be repressed.

*What was I thinking of staring at him when I accidentally walked into his room just as he was stepping out of the bathtub?*

She knew she should have turned away sooner, but instead, she stood frozen in place, allowing her eyes to take a full measure of the tall, handsome Adonis-like creature in all his glory. It was only his body's telling reaction that made her look away and finally run away as fast as she could down the long hall and out the door.

*What must he now think of me? From this moment on, all my pretense of being entirely unaffected by him must surely be for naught.*

Only a long solitary ramble about the park would do at such a time as that. Elizabeth walked and walked, and before she knew what she was about, she arrived at a magnificent stone temple. Situated amid wonderfully lush greenery, its haunting beauty arrested her eyes as well as her thoughts.

*Why! I never even knew such a place existed in the vicinity; else, I would have come long before now.*

In her haste to flee the manor house, Elizabeth had not donned her coat or her bonnet. She was beginning to feel the effect of her lapse. She wrapped her arms close to her bosom.

Despite the chilly air, she supposed she might as well continue walking toward the temple, for the thought of seeing Mr. Darcy so soon when the memory of every inch of his body from head to toes was so fresh in her mind was untenable.

Elizabeth swallowed a little. It was not so much his head or his toes that caused her to stir deep down inside. Rather, it was everything in between. His broad chiseled chest, his long legs, the arch of his sculptured pelvic muscles starkly defining his masculinity. The rousing manner in which one part of him sprang to life.

She could rightly say she had never seen anything like it before. At least not in real life, because pictures in the books her father and uncle kept in their libraries did not count.

By now, Elizabeth had arrived at the base of the temple, and she was about to ascend the stone stairs. Despite all the magnificence before her, Elizabeth's busy mind still lingered back at Rosings. She could never undo the act of seeing what she had seen, and truth be told, she had no wish to. If it were not for what such a desire might portend about Elizabeth's reputation, she was sure she wished to see it all again.

Elizabeth, upon reaching the top of the stairs, congratulated herself for continuing on to the temple, for now, the bright sun and the open landing conspired together against the chill in the air she had felt earlier, rendering it the perfect spot to sit and enjoy the sun against her face.

Elizabeth squatted by a high column, and leaning against it for support, shut her eyes. How heavenly it felt to be all alone as one with nature—so calm and peaceful with no one to disturb her. At length, she sat, crossed her legs, and breathed in the fresh air.

Elizabeth slowly drifted off to sleep, helpless in keeping her encounter with Mr. Darcy from creeping into her dreams.

*She was stepping out of her bath just as he entered her room - her bathing gown clinging to every inch of her body.*

*Coming to her in all his glory, he lifted her into his arms and carried her to the bed.*

*At length, the two lovers were no longer in Elizabeth's bed. They were at the temple instead. She was astride his body, calling out his name.*

*Mr. Darcy ... Mr. Darcy.*

*He adored her in every possible way that she wanted to be adored—all the while calling out her name.*

*Miss Bennet ... Miss Bennet.*

"Miss Bennet," she heard a gentleman say.

Startled, Elizabeth opened her eyes wide. She caught her breath. "Mr. Darcy! How long have you been here?"

"Not long. You were dreaming," Mr. Darcy said, crouching and sitting beside her. "Is it too much to wish for that you may have been dreaming of me?"

"Why?" Elizabeth asked, easing away from him a little. "Because of what I saw earlier? You flatter yourself, Mr. Darcy."

"Do I, Miss Bennet? I am rather certain I heard you calling out my name."

She shrugged. "If I were dreaming of you, which is not to say that I was, but if I were, then what of it? Am I not allowed? Or are such dreams entirely the prerogative of the male persuasion?"

"I see nothing wrong with a healthy curiosity."

"I must confess that I am more than a little curious about – certain things, but being a member of the gentler sex, I am obligated to wait until marriage to satisfy my curiosity, which is most inconvenient, for I am quite decided against marriage, at least in the foreseeable future." Elizabeth shrugged again. "Perhaps forever."

"Truly, Miss Bennet?" he asked, his tone containing a modicum of disbelief.

"What are you implying, Mr. Darcy?"

"I recall Lady Catherine mentioning Mr. Collins's intention of marrying the Bennet daughter of his choosing. I can only suppose he intends to choose you. I cannot help but notice how attentive he is toward you."

"I dare not argue your point, Mr. Darcy. The fact is, I know myself well enough to know that I could never marry such a ridiculous man. Still, my sister Mary supposes herself to be ideally suited to him, and as she is hoping they will make a match, I intend to do everything in my power to help them along. Now, hate me if you dare."

"Why would I hate you for doing what is in the best interest of your family? No, I applaud your efforts and even admire you so much more. It is a shame, though, that you have decided against marriage."

"I suppose you are a great proponent of marriage," Elizabeth said. "Have you any prospects, Mr. Darcy?"

"You are very blunt."

"I told you my secret - two of them, in fact, and now the least you can do is tell me yours."

"You did at that. I must confess to being more than a little intrigued - you have elaborated quite eloquently on your plans never to marry, but I confess I am far more intrigued by your other secret. I believe I might be of some service in that regard."

"I believe, sir, that you are changing the subject and rather indelicately."

"I am guilty as charged. To answer your question, I have no immediate prospects. However, there are those who think they know me who would argue otherwise."

"I'm listening," Elizabeth said, leaning closer.

"Lady Catherine's favorite wish is for me to marry Anne; however, it is never going to happen. I would sooner remain a single man - which I cannot afford to do because I am obligated to my family's legacy to beget an heir."

"Now, I am the one who is intrigued," Elizabeth said, arching her brow. "Pray, tell me more."

"What more is there to say?"

"Well, you said you will never marry Anne, and yet

Lady Catherine believes you will. That seems like a rather unenviable position to find oneself in. How do you plan to extricate yourself?"

"It is not as though I have not told my aunt as much. I suppose she will not really believe me until she reads about my engagement to another in the paper."

"I suppose that is one way to go about it, sir. No doubt, you will have no problem executing such a scheme. How hard will it be for you to find a bride?"

"I believe you would be quite surprised. Until recently, I had not met anyone with whom I might wish to form a lasting attachment, and then I suspected she was soon to be engaged to another."

"I am sorry to hear that, sir."

"Oh! You need not be, for I have it on excellent authority that she has no intention of marrying her would-be suitor, which means I might very well stand a chance. Which, by the way, brings me back to my earlier offer."

"Your earlier offer?"

"Indeed," Mr. Darcy said. "As regards your secret curiosity – specifically your dream that I believe I interrupted moments ago, as well as that which may or may not have been the source of its inspiration. I am more than happy to satisfy your curiosity."

Elizabeth reached out and tapped Mr. Darcy's hand. "How scandalous, sir. Why, if I did not know better, I would say you are a shameless flirt."

Darcy seized Elizabeth's hand and raised it to his lips. After brushing his lips against her hand, his tender gaze met her eyes. "Why would you say that, Miss Bennet?" He kissed her hand again. "Do you really suppose I am merely flirting with you."

Elizabeth's heart began beating so loudly that she could hear it. She swallowed. "Are you not, Mr. Darcy?"

"I am pleased to know that you are not bound to another man, and I am happy to show you just how pleased I am."

Elizabeth slowly withdrew her hand. "Sir, I fear you have an unfair advantage over me."

"How so?" he asked.

"You know all my secrets."

"Our secrets."

"No," Elizabeth said, standing. She was still rattled in the aftermath of having dreamed of lying in this man's arms and the disturbance in her composure of having been awakened by him. She needed to get away from him, the sooner the better.

"My secrets. Secrets that ought never to have been shared."

# CHAPTER 11

Mr. Collins had done nothing but pace the marble floor since his arrival, pausing only to stare out the window now and again, with his hands clasped behind his back. In his defense, he had been waiting for Elizabeth to join him in Lady Catherine's drawing-room for what seemed like hours. An inspection of either his pocket watch or the towering clock in the room would have told him that just under a half-hour had passed.

There Mary sat with a book in hand, a silent observer to it all.

At length, she said, "I am very sorry for my sister's delay, Mr. Collins."

"Is your sister often so inattentive as today's behavior suggests?" Collins asked, ceasing his pacing.

"Inattentive is not a word I would use to describe my sister. I do not know that our family would have gotten along half so well as we have, had it not been for Lizzy's steadfast determination to see us through. She will say that her dedication to our family's well-being is in keeping with our father's dying wish. However, anyone who really knows her, knows her commitment to our family goes much deeper than that. I am sure there is nothing she would not do for us that is within her power to do."

"Of course," said Mr. Collins, his tone containing a measure of contrition. "I did not mean to speak negatively about Cousin Elizabeth. Indeed, I am depending on her commitment to her family's well-being."

Mary, if she did not know when she agreed to join her sister on the trip to Kent, certainly knew by now that Mr. Collins preferred Elizabeth as the ideal companion of his future life. Mary also knew that if Elizabeth's marrying Mr. Collins was the only way to save her family from being tossed out of Longbourn, then her sister would surely marry him, even if doing so would cause both parties to be miserable.

And although Elizabeth had never confided as much to Mary, part of her suspected that Elizabeth knew exactly what she was about when it came to garnering Lady Catherine's good opinion. This was something Elizabeth wanted not for herself, but for Mary.

*I like Mr. Collins just as much now as ever before. Do I not owe it to myself as well as to my sister to seize the chance to be the true object of his affections?*

"I am certain she has lost herself in exploring the grounds."

"It seems your sister has a peculiar fondness for wandering about aimlessly. Indeed, there are far less taxing pursuits to be enjoyed by the female persuasion. Take yourself, for instance. When you are not reading a book, you are agreeably engaged practicing on the pianoforte. Indeed, both are particularly elegant pastimes for a gently bred young woman."

Her own pleasure aside, it was absolutely necessary to speak in her sister's defense. "You are aware of my sister's own penchant for reading, are you not, sir? Indeed, her love of reading far surpasses mine. As for her love of walking, I believe it is comparable to my love for music."

"Once again, you make an excellent point, Cousin Mary. Do you mind if I sit and talk with you while we wait for Cousin Elizabeth to return from her walk? Or perhaps we might take a turn about the grounds instead in the hope of meeting her."

"Sir, I would much prefer to remain indoors. Lady

Catherine has prognosticated rain this afternoon. And although there is nary a cloud in the sky, I should hate to ignore her prediction and find myself in a downpour. The last thing I want to do is chance being a burden."

"I am pleased to know how much you revere Lady Catherine's sage advice, Cousin," he uttered, drawing closer to where Mary sat.

"I would, however," Mary continued, "enjoy your company while we wait for Lizzy to return."

"I am pleased to hear you say that. What shall we do?"

"I have yet to practice today. Perhaps you might sit with me and turn the pages while I play."

"I cannot think of a better way to pass the time. Afterward, I might read Fordyce's sermons to you. Would you not like that?"

"I believe I should like that very much, Mr. Collins."

The gentleman rubbed his hands together in hearing this. "If your sister is lucky, she will have returned in time to join us. She will want to hear me reading Fordyce's just as much as you, I am sure."

If ever Mary were to criticize her sister Elizabeth, now would be the time. She could not think of a more disagreeable pastime, not only for Elizabeth but for any of her sisters.

*That is all the more reason for me to capture Mr. Collins's fancy. I have every reason to suppose we would be a most companionable couple indeed.*

# CHAPTER 12

*S*ir William Lucas had been formerly in trade in Meryton, where he had made a tolerable fortune, and risen to the honor of knighthood by an address to the king during his mayoralty. The distinction had perhaps been felt too strongly. It had given him a disgust to his business and his residence in a small market town. In quitting them both, he had removed with his family to a house about a mile from Meryton. He named his new abode Lucas Lodge. Unshackled by business, he occupied himself solely in being civil to all the world. Though elated by his rank, it did not render him supercilious. On the contrary, he was all attention to everybody.

His wife, Lady Lucas, was ideally suited to her husband's elevated status. What a triumph it was for her to be the first among her friends and neighbors to welcome the recently arrived Netherfield party to her home. Her husband, by virtue of his being the highest-ranking gentleman in the neighborhood, had been the first to call on Mr. Bingley.

With Lucas Lodge being so close in proximity to Longbourn, Lady Lucas and Mrs. Bennet suffered a relationship bordering on equal parts tolerance, familiarity, and one-upmanship. Both ladies had been burdened with several children. However, the former at least had a son to her credit, making her situation so much less troublesome than the latter's lot in life.

To Mrs. Bennet's way of thinking, the purpose of the evening's gathering was for the sole purpose of Lady Lucas's promoting her eldest daughter, Charlotte, to Mr. Bingley before the lady herself could do so. Mrs. Bennet was entirely persuaded that she would have been the first had Mr. Bennet not passed away when he did, for she would have insisted that he be the first to go to Netherfield to welcome the young man who reportedly had four or five thousand pounds a year.

Charlotte, being a sensible sort of young woman, summoned all her power not to be offended by Mrs. Bennet's constant disparagement about how much more suited her own daughters were for the rich, handsome gentleman.

As Charlotte and Elizabeth were the most intimate of friends, maintaining her composure as well as her civility in the wake of Mrs. Bennet's steady abuse was not an easy task. Still, she would not dare complain to her friend. Elizabeth, being a self-professed studier of people's character, was undoubtedly aware of her mother's deficits. She certainly needed no reminder from anyone.

Because of the intimate nature of the affair, only a half dozen or so families were included as guests that evening. There were Mr. and Mrs. Long and their two daughters. Mrs. Greene was in attendance, along with her nieces. Mr. and Mrs. King and their daughter Miss Mary King were there as well, along with the Goulds, a family with a healthy mix of sons and daughters. Last but not least were the Bennets: the aforementioned Mrs. Bennet, Miss Kitty Bennet, Miss Lydia Bennet, and Miss Bennet.

Miss Bennet, owing to her health, did not often have a chance to socialize. She never attended the local assemblies in Meryton, for instance, with all the boisterous clatter of people competing to be heard above the musicians, overcrowded dance floors, and often sweltering heat. What an unpleasant assault on

Jane's senses that would be. However, the convenience of a dinner party at the neighboring estate provided the ideal diversion. Yes, there was the steady hum of conversations taking place all about. However, being in the home of one of her closest friends afforded the ability of an easy escape if need be.

When, finally, the guest of honor and his party arrived, Sir William Lucas rushed to them. Charlotte, being a curious creature, hurried to her father's side. The youngest member of the party, whom Charlotte understood to be Mr. Charles Bingley, was good-looking and gentlemanlike. He had a pleasant countenance and easy, unaffected manners. The two women who accompanied him were very fine and possessed an air of decided fashion. The other man in the party merely looked the gentleman.

"Welcome to my humble abode, Mr. Bingley," said the host. "It is indeed a pleasure to have you and your family as our most honored guests."

Mr. Bingley smiled, rendering him even more charming in Charlotte's eyes.

"It is a pleasure being here, Sir William. I am sure I speak for all my family in expressing the utmost gratitude for your hospitality." The young man threw an astonished glance about the room. Charlotte could not help but notice the gentleman's eyes linger on

Jane before darting away. She certainly could not fault him, for none of the other young ladies were half so fair as Jane. Charlotte was sure that were it not for her affliction, Jane would have been married long ago.

"This is quite a gathering. I am looking forward to making everyone's acquaintance," Bingley offered.

"Indeed. I shall be delighted to introduce you to each and every one of my guests in turn. If you will allow me to do so, I should like to start with my lovely daughter, Charlotte. She is my eldest."

"Miss Lucas," said Mr. Bingley, bowing. "It is a pleasure to make your acquaintance. This is my brother-in-law and my sister, Mr. and Mrs. Hurst." After the refined couple acknowledged Charlotte in the usual way, Mr. Bingley continued. "And this is my sister Caroline."

"Miss Bingley," Charlotte said, with a slight curtsy. "It is a pleasure."

"I am sure," the young lady responded, her voice dismissive and her eye contact nonexistent.

What a striking contrast existed between the brother and sister. The former was everything that was amiable, and the latter presented herself as being above her company. Not that Charlotte cared, for that meant she would not have to give herself the trouble of speaking with the pretentious young lady for the rest of the evening.

Besides, Charlotte was much more interested in the brother, whose eyes were now fixed on Jane. By now, a line was forming by other guests who were anxious to meet the new neighbors, including Mrs. Bennet and her two younger girls. They had left Jane sitting alone on the sofa to fend for herself. Seeing this, Charlotte abandoned the spot she had staked beside her father and went to sit with her friend. She was more than happy to be Jane's eyes for the evening if that was what was required to assure the latter's comfort.

The next hours passed off pleasantly enough with most of the single young ladies busily engaged, at the encouraging of their eager mammas, vying for Mr. Bingley's attention. Charlotte was not one of them. She much preferred remaining by Jane's side, recounting what she would of what was happening all around.

"Tell me more about my new neighbors," Jane said. "I am sure you have exhausted the topic of Mr. Bingley himself, and I am convinced he is just what a young man ought to be."

Charlotte nodded in concurrence. "Indeed. He is sensible, good-humored, lively. I never saw such happy manners! He is so much at ease, with such perfect good breeding!"

"Yes—but what of his sisters?"

"Oh! I never saw two such miserable creatures in all my life. They look as though they would rather be any place but here. I imagine they must find our crude country manners rather appalling."

"Surely they are not so awful as that. Perhaps they are ill at ease when it comes to recommending themselves to strangers."

"That is precisely what I supposed you would say, dearest Jane. You never find fault in anyone. All the world is good, in your opinion."

"I fear you give me too much credit, dear Charlotte. It is not that I am incapable of finding fault in others; it is just that I dare not judge others too quickly lest I be judged myself and found wanting."

"I daresay nobody who really knows you would ever find you wanting, Jane."

"Now that is precisely what I supposed you would say. Next to Lizzy, you are my most ardent supporter." She held her hand out desiring Charlotte to claim it, which the latter did. Jane gave Charlotte's hand a gentle squeeze. "How can I thank you for remaining by my side this evening? I am sure I would not have enjoyed myself half so much were it not for you."

"Jane, you must know I will always be here for you as long as it is in my power. Soon enough, our dearest Lizzy shall return from Kent, and won't that be a cause for joy?"

Jane nodded and smiled. "Indeed. I can hardly wait for my sisters to return."

"Oh, my!" Charlotte cried, squeezing Jane's hand a little tighter.

"What is the matter?"

"Jane, my dear, I did not want to say anything before, but now I absolutely must, for I believe you have a most ardent admirer this evening."

"Oh, Charlotte, be serious."

"Indeed, I am very serious. There is a certain young man who has rarely taken his eyes off you since he entered the room. And you will never guess who he is."

"I am sure I have no idea. Pray, do you mean to keep me in suspense?"

"He is none other than Mr. Bingley," said Charlotte. "Heavens! I believe he is coming this way."

"What should I do?" Jane cried.

"Why! smile, of course."

---

The next morning, the manner in which the Netherfield party spoke of the gathering at Lucas Lodge was sufficiently characteristic of how each of them had behaved.

"I have never met with more pleasant people or prettier girls in my life," said Bingley. Had there been dancing, he was sure he would have danced with almost every maiden in the room, such was their eagerness in putting themselves forward. However, good food and delightful conversation were the order of the evening, a diverting combination that suited him just as well.

"You speak only for yourself, I am sure," cried Miss Caroline Bingley.

"Surely you jest, Caroline. Everybody was most kind and attentive to us." Indeed, for his part, there had been no formality or stiffness. By the end of the evening, he felt acquainted with all the room.

Miss Bingley scoffed. "I speak only the truth. But, of course, you would not have noticed the lack of good breeding and proper decorum that was so rampant. Thank heavens, Mr. Darcy was not there to witness such an appalling display."

Mrs. Hurst nodded. "I agree. I heard more than a few women speak of Charles's fortune, and what a good thing it would be if one of their daughters should make such an advantageous match. Can you imagine the manner of distraction that Mr. Darcy's presence would have been with his fortune of ten thousand pounds?"

"I grant you the hope of an advantageous alliance may very well have been the favorite wish of many of the young ladies in attendance. However, there was one among them who surely escaped such censure—Miss Bennet," Bingley asserted.

His heart slammed against his chest, merely saying her name out loud. Having kept her in his sights from the moment he first laid eyes on her, meeting her had been his primary objective, even as he attended everyone in his path who, unwittingly or not, stalled his efforts to do so. When at last, the way was clear, he strode directly over to where Miss Bennet sat and asked Miss Lucas for the pleasure of an introduction.

The look in Miss Bennet's eyes, the touch of her hand, and the sound of her voice told Bingley everything he needed to know. He could not conceive an angel more beautiful.

"Charles, I know your tendency to fall in love with every so-called angel you meet. But I thought surely in the eldest Bennet daughter's case, you would be sensible."

"Caroline!" Bingley exclaimed with energy.

The young woman held up her hand. "I grant you

that Miss Bennet is pretty enough. And, unlike that ridiculous mother and those silly sisters of hers, she seems intelligent enough. But for heaven's sake, Brother! Miss Bennet is not only penniless and, from what I overheard someone saying, is on the precipice of being uprooted from her home, but she is blind."

Bingley was no stranger to being on the opposite side of a heated debate with his youngest sister. But this time, Caroline had gone too far.

"Caroline, what on earth is the matter with you? Are you so insensitive to the sufferings of others? Did our own mother not suffer the same affliction as poor Miss Bennet? What sort of hypocrite would I be if I were to find fault in such an extraordinary creature because of her plight?"

Caroline swept her hand over her eyes and sighed. "My God, Charles!" Shaking her head, she opined, "Where in the world is Mr. Darcy when we need him?"

# CHAPTER 13

*E*lizabeth had learned a lesson about wandering the halls of the manor house while reading rather than paying attention to where she was going. That had not stopped her from doing so while walking about the park. On that morning, Elizabeth clutched her letter from her intimate friend, Charlotte, to her chest. She had committed one part, in particular, to her memory, having read it so often. Taking a seat on a bench, she read it in silence once more:

*"Oh, Lizzy! Wouldn't it be wonderful if Jane were to find happiness with Mr. Bingley? You and I both know Jane well enough to know she would never express such a sentiment out loud. Even your mother has not allowed herself to hope, and we know that if she thought an alliance between the*

gentleman and Jane were possible, she would not be able to keep it to herself. I, however, am not so constrained, and thus, I would shout it from the rooftop if I thought doing so would make such a felicitous prospect for Jane come true."

Elizabeth smiled. *Whoever this Mr. Bingley is, I can hardly wait to meet him.* Based on Charlotte's earlier letter, he was everything a gentleman ought to be, which was really saying something.

*The fact that he purportedly holds my Jane in such high esteem makes him a prince among men, in my estimation.*

Elizabeth wished for a first-hand account of this budding relationship from Jane herself. That would have to wait until the sisters were reunited. *Thank heaven, I have Charlotte to keep me informed.*

*Charlotte is not one to exaggerate, and she most assuredly would never entertain fanciful notions that have no basis in truth even if Mr. Bingley's acquaintance with my sister is of such short duration. Therefore, I must conclude that the possibility of Jane's finding the happiness she deserves is indeed a cause for hope.*

Elizabeth was roused from her reflections by someone's approach. More pleasure than she intended to show then overcame her, for it was none other than Mr. Darcy.

"I was hoping I would find you here," he said once he stood close enough to her.

"On such a lovely day as this, where else would I be, sir?"

"Indeed. May I join you?"

Nodding, Elizabeth made room on the bench for her most welcomed companion.

"As strange as this sounds, I had the most interesting conversation with Mr. Collins earlier."

She laughed a little. "I do not think I have ever heard the words 'interesting' and 'conversation' uttered together when speaking of Mr. Collins. Pray, tell me more." *What I find interesting is hearing those words coming from Mr. Darcy's mouth,* Elizabeth thought but did not say.

"Your point is well taken. That said, it looks like the two of us will be reunited soon after you take your leave of Kent."

"How do you suppose that, sir?"

"My friend, Charles Bingley, recently let Netherfield Park. I understand his estate is just three miles away from Longbourn. Indeed, I was meant to accompany him, but Lady Catherine required my presence here. I promised Bingley I would arrive in Hertfordshire once my aunt's business concerns allowed."

"What a coincidence that your friend is my new neighbor. What are the odds of our having first met here in Kent as opposed to Hertfordshire?"

"Some may call it fate."

"Fate, Mr. Darcy?"

"Indeed. One way or another, we were destined to be thrown into each other's path."

*Destiny, indeed.* Elizabeth was much happier that the two of them had met in Kent, rather than Hertfordshire. She liked Mr. Darcy very much, and she was sure the feeling was mutual. However, she was not so confident the two of them would have gotten along at all had they first met in Hertfordshire. True, Mr. Darcy was charming and amiable enough, but he barely tolerated Mr. Collins's ridiculousness.

*I can only imagine how he will comport himself with my mother and my two younger sisters. I have not the slightest doubt that the briefest time spent in company with the three of them will render my family severely wanting in Mr. Darcy's opinion.*

"That said," he continued, "knowing our paths are bound to cross again makes what I am about to say infinitely less painful. You see, Miss Bennet, I will be taking my leave of Kent in a matter of hours."

"What? So soon?"

"Yes, well, I have urgent business in town that requires my attention, and the colonel is eager to return as well."

Placing his hand on Elizabeth's chin, he gently

coaxed her to look into his eyes. "Is that a look of forlorn that I see?"

"You really do love to flatter yourself, Mr. Darcy," Elizabeth said, tearing her eyes away from his.

He urged her to look into his eyes once more. "Pray, be serious, Miss Bennet. I can assure you the look in my own eyes is utterly and completely one of forlorn. You cannot know what a pleasure it has been getting to know you. I do not mind confessing how much I shall miss spending time with you."

"I shall miss you too, Mr. Darcy," Elizabeth admitted. "You and the colonel, of course." The sudden change in his expression compelled Elizabeth to say more. "Especially you, sir." She smiled. "With whom else might I confide my secrets?"

"You can always write. I suspect you are very fond of letters," he said, eyeing the missive in her hand.

"Mr. Darcy!" Elizabeth exclaimed. "How scandalous! Surely you jest."

He shrugged. "What is one more secret between us?"

"I can assure you, sir, that is one secret you will never have to concern yourself with."

"No, I suppose you are correct. However, if you ever find yourself in need of anything, be it a willing listener or a shoulder to cry on, you must not hesitate to let me know. Promise me that you will."

"But, sir—"

He placed a finger on Elizabeth's lips, silencing her in the most tantalizing way. "Promise me."

Their eyes were fixed on each other's eyes. Mr. Darcy removed his finger, but his searing touch lingered still. Elizabeth felt as if they were the only two creatures in the world. At length, she whispered, "I promise."

Satisfied, Mr. Darcy took her hand into his and raised it to his lips. His kiss lingered. Elizabeth was lost to the amount of time that passed before he lowered her hand. "Until we meet again."

"Farewell, Mr. Darcy," she heard herself say, and she watched as he went away.

# CHAPTER 14

*W*ith her nephews' departure from Kent, Lady Catherine was now free to dwell on the matter of her remaining guests and their purpose for being in her home.

So far as she was concerned, the Bennet daughters were as different as night and day. Mr. Collins had been wise indeed to seek her opinion before taking such a drastic step. At five and twenty, he was still a young man. Far too young for the decades of misery incumbent with having chosen the wrong woman to be mistress of his new home and the mother of his children.

The time had come to render her verdict. There the two of them sat, alone in the drawing-room at Lady Catherine's beckoning.

"I hope for your sake, Mr. Collins, that Miss Mary is the Bennet daughter of your choice. She is nothing at all like her sister. Miss Elizabeth Bennet is not only impertinent, but she is far too opinionated for someone of her sphere. You would be miserable were you to be burdened by such a wife," said her ladyship. "That is to say nothing about her unbecoming habit of traipsing about the countryside. Such a partner in life would surely reflect poorly on any man, especially one such as yourself, whose prospects are so bright."

"As you know, Lady Catherine, I would never make such a decision on whom I ought to marry without first obtaining your blessing. I, too, find certain shades in my cousin Elizabeth's character to be wanting. Whereas, the more time I spend getting acquainted with Cousin Mary, the more I value her many lovely qualities."

"I, for one, am glad to hear you speak that way. One would be blind not to see that Miss Mary Bennet was designed for you. As for her sister, with such an impertinent disposition as hers, she will likely never marry a gentleman of any real consequence in the world. With any luck, she will seek a position as a governess, although I do not know who would employ her. Alas, she, along with her mother and sisters, will remain a burden to you until you can find someone to take one or another of them off your hands."

"Indeed, your ladyship. However, such is a lot in life I shall gladly endure."

"Well then, away with you. Go and share your happy news with Miss Mary with my blessings. Though you will not be the wealthiest gentleman in the country, all that you will have is certainly no less than you deserve."

---

Next, it was Mr. Collins's turn to have a private audience with another member of the Rosings party.

"Pray have a seat, Cousin Elizabeth, for I fear you will want to be seated when you hear what I have to say."

Recalling that she had been seated at the table when Mr. Collins initially offered his hand to her at Longbourn, Elizabeth felt her stomach turn. What's more, both of his hands were behind his back. If he offered her a flower or some other token of his affection, she feared she might bolt from the room.

*No,* she thought to herself. *Such rashness on my part would never do.*

"What on earth is this about, Mr. Collins?" Elizabeth demanded. Her waning patience mixed with dread was evident in her voice.

"Trust me when I say you will want to be seated for this."

Elizabeth folded one arm over the other. "Trust me when I say, I have no intention of sitting so long as you keep me in suspense."

Collins shook his head and clasped his hands - his empty hands - in front of him. "Very well, but prepare yourself to be quite disheartened. However, I do suspect, or at least I hope your disappointment will be of a short duration once you have had time to digest my news."

Now Elizabeth was beginning to worry. She feared that Lady Catherine might have persuaded the man against either Bennet daughter. Then where would her family be?

*Mr. Collins will toss us out into the hedgerows for sure.*

"I am listening," Elizabeth said in a voice impatient for Mr. Collins to continue his speech.

"You cannot have missed the growing camaraderie between your sister Cousin Mary and me during our time here in Kent. What we have shared has progressed from what was at first akin to brotherly and sisterly affection for each other into something more meaningful, more lasting - dare I say it aloud, in a word, love."

Elizabeth's eyes opened wide. If she did not dislike Mr. Collins as much as she did, she would have wrapped her arms around him in jubilation. Instead, she took a seat, which was encouragement enough for Mr. Collins to sit as well.

Keeping her joy under wraps, Elizabeth sat there. She stared. She celebrated in silence. She said nothing.

"I can tell by your solemn expression how this must surely affect you, and that is why I have not uttered a word of my intentions to your sister. I believe it is my duty as a gentleman to speak with you first, especially because I know you had counted on being the Bennet daughter of my choosing. I rather hope you will look beyond your own disappointment and see fit to release me from the peculiar arrangement we entered into before coming to Kent with the hope of getting Lady Catherine's blessings."

He regarded Elizabeth in all earnestly. "We both agreed, did we not, that Lady Catherine's blessings would be absolutely necessary for us to proceed? You do remember?"

"Of course, I remember," Elizabeth said, breaking

her silence and even feigning a bit of disappointment for good measure.

"I ought to mention that I did, indeed, obtain Lady Catherine's blessing. However, it was not to marry you, but rather your sister. Both her ladyship and I agree that such a union will contribute greatly to my chances for felicity in marriage. Cousin Mary satisfies my every wish for what I desire most in the companion of my future life."

"Yet, you have not spoken with my sister about any of this," Elizabeth responded.

"No, I have not. I was determined to do nothing until I spoke with you. I have every reason to suppose your sister will accept my hand in marriage, but only if she knows that doing so does not come at the expense of your own happiness."

"What are you saying, sir?"

"What I am saying or rather asking is for your blessing for an alliance between your sister and me. Only if I have your support will I embark upon this path."

"Sir, I do not know quite what to say."

"Say I have your blessing as well as your permission to press my suit with your sister."

Elizabeth nodded. "Yes, yes. Of course, you do - on both accounts. Having seen the two of you grow closer these past days and weeks, I would be the last person in the world to stand in your way."

Mr. Collins rose from his seat. "You have my deepest gratitude for your sacrifice, Cousin Elizabeth. I am forever in your debt. Now, if you will excuse me, I am most eager to seek out your sister." With that, he headed toward the door.

"Mr. Collins," Elizabeth said, causing the gentleman to halt. "I would ask you but one thing in return."

"What is that, for I am more than happy to oblige?"

"Simply this," Elizabeth replied. "Do anything but disappoint my sister. Always be there for her, placing her needs above those of all other mortal beings. It is nothing less than she deserves."

Elizabeth did manage to wait until Mr. Collins had quit the room before she danced about in happiness and triumph. She wanted to share her elation with the one person in the world with whom she had confided her scheme. She wanted to tell Mr. Darcy, and she meant to do it. But then it dawned on her.

*Mr. Darcy is not here. He is off in London or in other parts unknown. For all I know, he may even be in Hertford-shire by now.*

At least this last thought gave her a modicum of comfort. She knew not when she would see Mr. Darcy again, but one thing was certain. She would indeed see him again.

*I can hardly wait.*

---

Mary sat alone in Lady Catherine's library. The words on the page blurred before her, for matters of a different kind occupied her busy mind. Just when she contemplated putting aside her book, the object of her musings entered the room.

"I have just come from a private audience with your sister," Mr. Collins declared.

By his expression, the gentleman looked as if he had happy news to convey, and oddly enough, he appeared to expect Mary to concur. But if what the gentleman had to say was what Mary expected, then how could she possibly be happy?

Still, Mary laid the book she was reading aside and, without speaking, waited patiently for the gentleman to continue his speech.

"Indeed, I have news that is certain to please everyone."

For the first time in her life, Mary suffered feelings akin to heartbreak. *Oh, why, oh, why did I subject myself to such pain as this? I should have known Mr. Collins would choose Lizzy.*

Her consolation was the knowledge that her own chances had been based on the slightest of possibilities. *I do not know that I would have forgiven myself had I not tried.*

Still, she had allowed herself to hope, and the threat of suffering any measure of agony was more than she wished to bear. Almost on the verge of bolting from her seat, she watched in amazement as Mr. Collins lowered himself to one knee.

Tears one might expect from a love-struck girl pooled in her eyes.

Mr. Collins thus began. "I believe it is only fair to inform you that upon first meeting your family, though it was always my intention to choose a bride from among the Bennet daughters as a means of making amends for the misfortune of the entail on the Longbourn estate, my vanity overruled my reason in forming an opinion on which of you ought to be the companion of my future life.

"However, as a consequence of our being here in Kent, my eyes and indeed my heart have conspired," he went on the say. "Indeed, together, they have thus informed me of who my ideal choice must surely be.

That person, my dear Cousin Mary, is you. Your modesty, your economy, your natural delicacy, and most importantly, your keen sense of how a proper young lady ought to be are such that I am convinced you are the only Bennet daughter capable of contributing to my felicity.

"What is more, your demonstration of reserve and deference that Lady Catherine de Bourgh's rank inevitably excites speaks to your suitability as well. Indeed, it is with her ladyship's blessing that I present myself to you on bended knee with an offer of my hand in marriage."

Mr. Collins's words, though not elegant, were precisely the words Mary wished to hear, and she expressed herself as sensibly as a young woman of her temperament could be expected to do.

The happiness which this reply produced was such as Mr. Collins had probably never felt before, encouraging him to conclude his speech by saying, "It seems nothing remains for me but to assure you in the most animated language of the violence of my affection."

At last, Miss Mary Bennet could proclaim her happiness was all but complete. What was more, she was to be the first of her sisters to suffer such a pleasure. Unlike her sisters, Mary had long fancied herself as being far too sensible to expect a love match, and yet she supposed she had it.

*Our family is saved, and I know precisely who to thank for our good fortune.*

She could hardly wait to speak to her sister and then to write to her mother. But first, there was the matter of the violence of affections that Mr. Collins had promised.

*Surely that is the most pressing order of the moment.*

# CHAPTER 15

*M*ere days later, Lady Catherine was livid. How dare her nephew Darcy return to Rosings Park so soon after his departure. What is more, he had made it perfectly clear that his reason for returning had nothing to do with his obligation to Anne.

On the contrary, Darcy had attempted once again to disavow his obligation to fulfill the favorite wish of Lady Catherine and his own mother, the late Lady Anne Darcy, that the cousins were to be married. From their cradles, the two cousins were destined for each other – an advantageous union like no other.

If he was not there to spend time with Anne, and he was not there on Lady Catherine's behest, then what possible reason could he have for returning as soon as he did?

Her ladyship did not have to ponder the question for very long before she knew beyond the shadow of a doubt what was afoot.

From her vantage point, staring out the window overlooking her maze garden, the evidence was plain to see. Mr. Darcy and Miss Bennet walked along beside each other, standing much too close for Lady Catherine's taste.

*I mean to put an end to my nephew's trifling affection for that impertinent Miss Elizabeth Bennet for once and for all. Merely banishing her from my home will not suffice. I must guarantee that young chit is forever beyond my nephew's reach.*

---

An hour or so later, lady Catherine was sitting in her parlor being attended by Mr. Collins, who even now performed the role of a most loyal subject.

"I fear I may have been premature in recommending that you choose Miss Mary Bennet instead of her sister," she said.

Mr. Collins shifted in his seat but remained silent.

"I do not like to admit when I have been wrong, a

consequence of rarely exhibiting such human frailty, no doubt, but I suppose it happens to the best of us. Fortunately, this mistake is easily rectified."

"I am afraid I am not following you, your ladyship. Through no fault of your own, of course. The failing is completely mine."

"Then, you can have no doubt of what is to be done." Lady Catherine did not wait for a response. She had no reason to do so. If anyone on earth would do her bidding, it was Mr. Collins. "You must marry Miss Elizabeth Bennet."

"I beg your pardon, Lady Catherine. You are aware, are you not, that Cousin Mary and I are engaged to be married. She has written to her family to share the happy news."

Her ladyship reared her regal head. "What is that to me, or you either, for that matter? I have rescinded my blessing to such an alliance and conferred it instead to a union between you and Miss Elizabeth Bennet."

Collins shook his head. "I am afraid it is too late for that."

"How dare you speak to me in such a manner!" she exclaimed. "Is the entire reason for the Bennet daughters being here not to garner my opinion on which one you ought to marry? Well, now you have it, and I expect you to act accordingly."

"True, my coming here to seek your blessing for an alliance between a Bennet daughter and me was indeed the principal reason. I am thankful for it; else, I would have made a grave mistake so far as my future happiness is concerned.

"Marrying Cousin Elizabeth would very well cause me to suffer from misery of the acutest kind. Of that, I am convinced without a single shred of a doubt. Not because of any fault in her character, mind you, but because she and I are as different as night and day, whereas Cousin Mary seems to be designed for me. She and I have but one mind and one way of thinking. There is, in everything, a most remarkable resemblance of character and ideas between us.

"I have offered her my hand in marriage, and she has graciously accepted. So far as I am concerned, we are as good as husband and wife. I have promised to protect her, to have and to hold her, and to place no one else above her. I shall allow no one to cast our imminent union asunder. Not even you, Lady Catherine. I am sorry it disappoints you, but this is how I feel."

"And this is your final resolve? This is how you intend to express your gratitude to me after all I have done for you. In view of how much I can do for you still - opening doors that would otherwise be closed to you. Do you realize it is in my power to see that you are not received in any decent home?"

"That may very well be true, and I hope you will think better of your threat. However, as the master of my own estate with a wife and a family to call my own, I'm sure I can have no cause to repine."

# CHAPTER 16

*H*aving learned from his valet that the Bennet daughters were preparing for their immediate departure from Kent, Mr. Darcy instructed the man to deliver a message to the eldest Miss Bennet. He requested that she meet him in the east wing. Nobody used that part of the manor house. Thus, their privacy was assured.

Not a quarter-hour later, the aggrieved gentleman paced the floor. Running his hand through his hair, he proclaimed, "This is my fault."

Indeed, after listening to Elizabeth's account on why she and Mary were taking their leave of Kent so suddenly, he was sure this was his aunt's way of seeking retribution against him.

"Why would you possibly blame yourself, Mr. Darcy?"

"Because your leaving has everything to do with my returning to Kent. I came back to see you, Miss Bennet. I had to see you, and Lady Catherine knows it."

"I am afraid I do not understand."

"No, I do not expect you do. The fact is, I can hardly understand it myself. All I know is that I wanted to see you again, even though I know that you and I would be in each other's company in Hertford-shire in a matter of weeks."

Such had been what his cousin the colonel had argued upon learning of Darcy's intention to return to Kent. Darcy's desire to be with Elizabeth would not be repressed, nor would it be pacified by the promise of a future reunion at some unspecified time.

"I hope you do not mind my telling you this," he offered. "I know our acquaintance is of rather short duration, but I like spending time with you. It is my hope that you feel the same."

"I do."

"And I hope you will allow me to make amends for my aunt's poor hospitality."

"What do you have in mind, sir?"

"Allow me to take you and your sister away from Kent to Hertfordshire."

"I suppose there is no harm in your proposal, so long as you do not forget Mr. Collins."

"Mr. Collins?"

"Indeed. Have you not heard the happy news? There is soon to be a wedding in my family."

"Tell me your mission to persuade the gentleman to transfer his ardent attention to your sister bore fruit."

"It did indeed. I do not know which of us is happier, my sister Mary or me."

"I am happier for you, but then again, I am biased. Or need I remind you?"

"No reminder is needed, sir. I am sure I will never forget, which begs the question - are you sure I am safe accepting your generous offer? I am not in the habit of being in anyone's debt."

"No, you are far too independent for that. However, even the most independent-minded of us can not object to the service of a friend."

Her feelings divided between hope and uncertainty, Elizabeth asked, "Is that what we are, Mr. Darcy? Friends?"

"Are we not?"

She pursed her lips. "Can members of the opposite sex be friends?"

"That I cannot say. Nor can I say where a friendship between the two of us may or may not lead. But I cannot think of a greater foundation than we currently have from which to make a start. Agree?"

"I agree."

"Then let us get you away from this place."

"As inclined as I am to accept your offer, Mr. Darcy, I do not know that I am at liberty to do so. Now that Mr. Collins and my sister are engaged, he is as good as the head of our family. Only the want of a marriage decree will make his new role official."

The gentleman nodded his head. "I know you well enough to know this is a change that will take some getting used to on your part."

"Indeed," Elizabeth replied. "Not that I would have it any other way. Were it within my power, I would rather the marriage occur by a special license. My family's place at Longbourn has been marred by uncertainty for far too long."

"Certainly," Mr. Darcy said, "if such an arrangement is mutually agreed to by your cousin, I am willing to do everything in my power to help bring it about."

"No, such speculation is merely wishful thinking

on my part. It is not for me to say how my sister's marriage should come about."

"Of course, you are correct. That said, I will go to the Parsonage house to extend the invitation to travel to Hertfordshire in the Darcy carriage. I am sure it is an offer your cousin will not wish to refuse."

Elizabeth smiled a little at the thought of what Mr. Collins's response to Mr. Darcy's offer would be. In view of the fact that the gentleman's standing in Lady Catherine de Bourgh's esteem had effectively vanished, he would relish a chance to have the nephew stand by him instead.

*As a young man who is coming into his own, Mr. Collins can have no doubt that Mr. Darcy has far more to offer.*

---

The eventual arrival at Longbourn in the company of none other than Lady Catherine de Bourgh's nephew did not arouse the degree of suspicion and innuendo that such an occasion might otherwise call for. It stood to reason, after all, that Lady Catherine would prevail on her relation to extend such a courtesy to her guests. As Mr. Darcy was already going to Hertfordshire to visit his friend Charles Bingley, the Bennet sisters would be in nobody's way.

Elizabeth's family, specifically her mother, did not need to know the actual circumstances of her daughters' departure from Rosings Park. Certainly, none of the affected parties were likely to boast of their exodus. On the other hand, Mrs. Bennet did not seem to care. Her daughter Mary's engagement to the heir of Longbourn would be the means of the Bennets' remaining in their home, or as she proclaimed with glee, "We are saved!"

Mrs. Bennet did, however, insist upon Mr. Darcy's taking a family dinner with them. She easily surmised that any friend of Mr. Bingley's must surely be rich, but she could have no way of knowing the wide disparity in the gentlemen's wealth. Even though her mother always had an excellent table – despite all Elizabeth's attempts to inject a greater sense of economy into the household after her father's passing - Elizabeth could not be sure how Mr. Darcy would comport himself among those who were so far beneath him in consequence. She had borne witness to the degree of his fastidiousness while traveling with him. They had changed horses at least three times during their hurried journey, and rarely did the gentleman bother taking much sustenance.

Were it not for her having spent so much time with him as she had in Kent, Elizabeth would not have recognized Mr. Darcy. He had donned a mask of indifference that belied everything she knew about him. As it turned out, all her worry of having to shield Longbourn's illustrious visitor from the notice of her mother and her youngest sisters, all of whom feared his conversing with would cause the gentleman utter mortification, had been in vain.

# CHAPTER 17

*D*arcy's late arrival at Netherfield, the night before, followed by his early rise that morning, allowed him to elude Miss Caroline Bingley's company a while longer. He had no doubt how eager the young lady must be to see him.

For the time being, his time was better spent with his friend Bingley touring the estate. After a lengthy excursion on horseback, the two returned to the manor house at a rather leisurely pace.

"Netherfield is a fine place, Charles. Even as a tenant, I imagine you will suffer immense pride in residing at such a place is this."

Bingley's face beamed. "I am relieved to know you approve. I admit to having suffered some doubt in that regard. Your good opinion is not easily bestowed."

Darcy frowned. "I would like to think I am not so fastidious as you suggest."

The younger man shrugged. "I suppose you have undergone a metamorphosis of sorts. Who would have supposed that you of all people would have formed an acquaintance with my country neighbors? I do not suppose your aunt Lady Catherine de Bourgh approves of your having such connections. I recall your having met the two Bennet daughters at Rosings Park, did you not?"

"In truth, my aunt does not approve of anyone who does not readily bend to her will, regardless of one's station in life. She and I were bound to come to a parting of the ways once I made it perfectly clear to her that my cousin Anne and I are never going to be married."

Bingley laughed a little. "So far as my sister Caroline is concerned, she never suffered a shred of doubt in that regard. She clings to the hope that your future lies with her."

Darcy scoffed. "Pray, do not remind me."

"I do not suppose she will be pleased knowing that you and the Bennets are already acquainted. Her greatest wish, aside from claiming your heart for herself, is that you will prevail on me to see the error of my ways."

"What do you mean? Is she still so opposed to your letting the estate?"

Bingley nodded. "Well, there is that. There is also the matter of my feelings for Miss Jane Bennet." The younger man exhaled a long breath. "You mentioned having dined with her family. Do you not agree that she is an angel?"

Darcy suffered no surprise in hearing his friend speak this way. Miss Bennet was indeed lovely – just the sort of angel with whom Bingley had a habit of falling in love.

Not wanting to point out the many things Caroline Bingley, no doubt, had used in her own arguments against her brother once again falling in love, Darcy said, "Yes, I must confess she is very pretty. As are all the Bennet sisters - in their own way, of course."

"I have heard it said that Miss Elizabeth is the brightest jewel in the country, in beauty as well as in intellect. I can hardly wait to meet her. Shall we call on Longbourn this morning?"

As much as Darcy wanted to see Elizabeth, he could not quite say the same for other members of her family. The hours spent in close confines with Mr. Collins on the journey from Kent to Longbourn had taught him just how fortunate Elizabeth was to have escaped such an alliance.

Making matters worse, the gentleman had presumed an acquaintance with Darcy that in any other circumstance would be deemed inconceivable.

Then there was the matter of Elizabeth's mother and her two younger sisters. Darcy had no choice but to don a mask of haughtiness mixed with aloofness with Mrs. Bennet. Else, he was sure she would have overwhelmed him with her adoration and affected approbation, the likes of which he had received from every other eager mamma, with a single daughter in want of a rich husband, whom he had ever met.

As for the younger sisters, they were two of the silliest creatures in all of England. Elizabeth had warned him as much on more than one occasion. He thought she was exaggerating.

*If only she were.*

During the limited time he spent in company with them, he was convinced the wild, untamed spirits of the younger and the fickle mindedness of the other were the perfect recipe for a scandal in the making. He prayed his instincts were wrong.

The sooner Miss Mary Bennet married Mr. William Collins, the sooner the Bennet family's burdens would be relieved, and the sooner Miss Elizabeth could dedicate herself to her own happiness.

*Her happiness with me,* part of him silently considered even if he was not quite ready to admit it to the part of himself that knew better than to fall in love too soon.

Darcy said, "As much as I might wish to delay my imminent reunion with your family, I did not suppose I would ever hear the end of it if I did not make an appearance at breakfast this morning. I am afraid our calling on Longbourn must wait."

---

"What do you mean you are already acquainted with my brother's neighbor?" Miss Caroline Bingley inquired after hearing about the circumstances of Darcy's arrival in Hertfordshire. "How is such a thing even possible, and why on earth have I heard nothing of this before now?"

"I met Miss Elizabeth and Miss Mary Bennet when we were all in Kent," was Darcy's reply. "They were guests at my aunt's home."

"Why! I had no idea the Bennets enjoyed such lofty connections!" she exclaimed with energy. "Having met them, I can scarcely believe it. I have never met with anyone so uncouth, so ill-mannered, so wanting. That mother of theirs is an abomination. If it were not for her being as blind as she is to my brother's trifling infection with her eldest, I dare say she would be planning a wedding here at Netherfield as we speak."

"Caroline!" Bingley exclaimed, no doubt concerned that his sister would once again cite Miss Bennet's blindness as a reason to consider her wanting.

Caroline paid her brother no mind. "No doubt, Mrs. Bennet will be throwing her next eldest daughter at Charles now that she has returned. What can you tell me about the second one, Mr. Darcy?"

Setting aside his cup of piping hot coffee, Darcy cleared his throat. "Having spent significant time in Miss Elizabeth's company, I would have to say she is one of the most handsome, most intelligent, and most charming women of my acquaintance."

It was now Miss Bingley's turn to set her cup aside. Picking up her linen napkin, she brushed it against her lips. "My goodness. I am all astonishment," she then replied. "Such a glowing assessment as that begs the question - pray, when am I to wish you joy?"

That was precisely the question which he had expected Miss Bingley to ask. Her own infatuation with him had not abated one bit in all the time he had known her, even though he had done nothing to encourage her.

"I knew you would be wishing me joy," he said without admitting his purpose in putting her on notice as regarded his opinion of Miss Elizabeth Bennet.

"And to think mere moments earlier you were positing an alliance between Charles and this intriguing Miss Elizabeth Bennet," opined Mr. Hurst, taking everyone by surprise what with his preference to avoid such contentious banter. He had much rather keep himself to himself.

"Hush, Brother-in-law," Caroline demanded. "I am waiting to hear a more definitive reply from our Mr. Darcy."

"Let me just say this, Miss Bingley. When the time comes to be wishing me joy, I am sure you will be among the first to know. No, make that among the second to know."

# CHAPTER 18

*H*ome again. How wonderful it felt to utter two of the sweetest sounding words to Elizabeth's ear. That her family's fate was all but secured, what with the imminent wedding between Mary and Mr. Collins, Elizabeth suffered sentiments akin to elation in saying them. At long last, the fear of the unknown as regarded the estate was gone, never to be thought of again. At least, she hoped so. She silently lamented neither Mr. Collins's nor Mary's broaching the possibility of a marriage by special license.

*Now that Mr. Collins and my sister are engaged, time is of the essence.* Whether by adherence to decorum or by his character, Elizabeth's future brother-in-law intended to stay in the inn in Meryton until the happy occasion.

*At least there is that.*

She really wanted the wedding to be over and done with, for she could not help but dread the possibility, however minuscule, that something might happen to derail the scheme. What that might be, Elizabeth had no idea. All she knew was nothing was really certain until it was indeed certain. During such times, she reminded herself that Mr. Collins was still a young man, and as best she could tell, he was the epitome of good health, as was her sister Mary. She worried not that an untimely death might upset things.

*Soon enough, the Banns will be read, and our family's happiness will be complete, and my tacit promise to my father to see to my family's wellbeing will be satisfied. I really do like to think I have done my best by my family since Papa's passing. Mary's impending nuptials are the icing on the cake.*

In the meantime, reacquainting herself with the goings-on in Hertfordshire was uppermost in Elizabeth's mind. So much had happened since she and Mary went away to Kent, the most auspicious occasion of all, of course, being the arrival of the Netherfield party. Charlotte had done an admirable job of keeping Elizabeth abreast of the newcomers and all their predilections. Still, nothing could take the place of meeting the infamous Mr. Bingley and his peculiar relations for oneself.

The matter of the Bingleys was the object of discussion that very day. Elizabeth, Jane and Charlotte were all present. An air of nostalgia-filled the room, as warm and cheery as ever before.

Charlotte said, "Dearest Lizzy, I am more than happy to espouse on the amiable Mr. Charles Bingley and his pernicious sisters, Mrs. Louisa Hurst and Miss Caroline Bingley. But first, I must insist upon your telling us all there is to know about Mr. Bingley's friend, Mr. Darcy."

It appeared word had spread throughout the neighborhood at a much quicker pace than Elizabeth would have preferred that Mr. Darcy, the very wealthy and often heralded imminent addition to the Netherfield party, had finally arrived in Hertfordshire with the Bennet sisters in tow. What could it mean, everyone would want to know, or so Elizabeth supposed.

Even Elizabeth was hard-pressed to supply an answer. There was much that she might tell were she indeed capable of finding the right words. Would anyone honestly believe that in bringing them to Hertfordshire, the gentleman had merely been serving the role of a friend?

"It is a testament to the fact that it is indeed a small world," Elizabeth replied, much the same as she intended to do whenever she was asked about the scheme. "Mary and I met Mr. Darcy in Kent when we were all guests at his aunt Lady Catherine de Bourgh's home. You can imagine our surprise upon learning that Mr. Darcy was connected to our new neighbors at Netherfield Park. I suppose it only made sense for him to offer to bring us along to Hertfordshire, thus sparing us the expense as well as the inconvenience of a public coach."

Charlotte said, "I suspect you are concealing far more than you are revealing, dearest Lizzy. However, I shall not press you to say more. Time has a way of satisfying such curiosities, after all. Perhaps there shall be three weddings here at Longbourn in the not too distant future."

Elizabeth laughed a little at her friend's conjecture. "Oh, there will be at least one wedding to be sure. I would not count on a second if you suppose it will occur between Mr. Bingley's friend, Mr. Darcy, and me. As for a supposed third, what on earth are you suggesting, dear Charlotte?"

Jane, who had been silent for the most part, said, "I am afraid Charlotte is positing an alliance between Mr. Bingley and me."

Elizabeth's eyes opened wide. "Oh, Jane! Pray such speculation is well-founded. I know I have yet to make Mr. Bingley's acquaintance, but given all I have heard, he seems the consummate gentleman."

"If Charlotte is the source of your intelligence, I can well imagine all you have been told about Mr. Bingley," said Jane.

"I have told Lizzy nothing but the truth. Mr. Bingley is everything the heart desires, and best of all, he is utterly smitten with our Jane."

Jane did not appear nearly so convinced of Mr. Bingley's affection as did Charlotte, as her subsequent protests attested, but on the other hand, Jane rarely showed her true feelings. Elizabeth feared such reticence on Jane's part was merely a means of protecting herself from the pang of disappointed hopes. Bearing witness to Jane's sufferings broke Elizabeth's heart. Her elder sister was everything that was good in Elizabeth's estimation. Her outer beauty paled in comparison to her inner beauty, which was really saying something. Elizabeth was sure she would give anything to see her sister happy.

All along, Elizabeth clung to the hope that Jane's vision might one day return. It was not out of the question that her sight would be restored just as suddenly and inexplicably as it had faded. All the books that Elizabeth had read on the subject had taught her to hope as much, and even the physician Jane had seen as a child had not ruled out such a possibility.

Elizabeth reached for her sister's hand and cradled it inside both of her own. "All I can say is this, Jane. If even half of what Charlotte says is true," here she turned to her friend and spoke apologetically, "and dear Charlotte, you know I mean you no harm, nor do I doubt you." She returned her attention to Jane. "I have yet to meet this Mr. Bingley, but I wager he would have to be a fool if he is not half in love with you already."

Later that same day, Elizabeth met the amiable Charles Bingley when he called on Longbourn with Mr. Darcy in tow. Now was her chance to observe first-hand the growing affection that Charlotte had witnessed on Mr. Bingley's part toward Jane.

How delighted Elizabeth was that her mother, Kitty, and Lydia were away when the gentlemen called. Even the recently betrothed Mary and Mr. Collins were nowhere to be found. The housekeeper had attributed their absence to Mr. Collin's wish to see the view from Oakham Mount.

Once all the usual civilities inherent in such an occasion ebbed, Mr. Bingley seemed impatient for diversion. "Did I not hear you express your admiration of the garden on one side of the lawn when we entered the gate, Darcy?" said he to his friend.

Without awaiting a response, Bingley added, "It is much too pleasant to remain indoors. Perhaps we might take a turn in it." He gazed at Jane. "What say you, Miss Bennet?"

"I shall be delighted with your company, sir." Jane turned toward her sister. "Shall we be favored with your company as well, Lizzy? That is to say, yours and Mr. Darcy's?"

Knowing how much her sister enjoyed spending time in the garden with the sun beaming down on her, Elizabeth was glad for Mr. Bingley's suggestion. She could not be sure of what Mr. Darcy wanted, for he had rarely spoken in anything but monosyllables since his arrival.

Seeing the two gentlemen together, Elizabeth could hardly imagine why they were such good friends. Their temperaments were nothing alike.

Elizabeth could not help but notice that Mr.

Darcy's attention was frequently drawn by his friend as well as by Jane. The evening before, he had paid no more attention to her elder sister than he had to Kitty or Lydia.

His silent scrutiny continued after the four of them made their way to the garden when Mr. Bingley and Jane sat beside each other on a wooden bench. Elizabeth could not help but wonder if Mr. Darcy's seeming interest in Jane was a consequence of something he had learned from either Mr. Bingley or perhaps the young man's family.

Elizabeth feared the latter might have poisoned Mr. Darcy's mind against Jane. Though she had yet to meet the Bingley sisters, Charlotte had told Elizabeth enough about the two of them to teach her to be circumspect where their motives were concerned.

In truth, Bingley's sisters and how they may or may not feel about her family meant nothing to Elizabeth. She did, however, care about Mr. Darcy's opinion. She surmised Mr. Darcy exercised prodigious care over his friend, hence his being in Hertfordshire to aid him with the ins and outs of estate management.

*One word from Mr. Darcy might very well extinguish his friend's growing admiration for Jane.*

Elizabeth's busy mind settled when she espied Mr.

Bingley present Jane with a bouquet of flowers that he had gathered along the way. Jane held the gay assortment to her nose and breathed in deeply. She smiled.

Elizabeth's happiness in seeing such joy in her sister's face was complete.

## CHAPTER 19

*L*ydia's incessant wailing flooded the halls. One had to be deaf not to hear her. Mrs. Bennet, Mary, and Jane were visiting the Lucases that morning, which left only Kitty and Elizabeth to comfort the poor child.

"Lydia!" Elizabeth exclaimed with energy. "What on earth is the matter?"

"I do not wish to marry that decrepit old man," Lydia cried. "I am too young to die!"

"Too young to die. What are you talking about, Lydia? Since when is getting married synonymous with dying? But more important than that, who has proposed to you?"

"That horrid Mr. Coble is demanding that I marry him or else!" Lydia replied. She looked at Elizabeth through tear-filled eyes. "He said I owe him my hand in marriage because of all the things he has given me these past weeks. But why would I marry such a man? Especially now, when I know what I know!

"Am I to pretend to be ignorant of all the talk about his three previous wives? Am I to pretend to be ignorant of the reason behind his horrible nickname?"

Kitty said, "Indeed. I am sure Mr. Coble is not known as the *'merry'* widower for nothing!"

Elizabeth was indeed privy to the rumors widely circulated at the times of Mr. Coble's previous wives' deaths. As nothing was ever proved, soon enough, the stories died too. Whether the gentleman's wealth and connections had anything to do with anything was not for the people of Meryton to say.

Elizabeth supposed Lydia might have never heard the hushed whispers surrounding the man upon first making his acquaintance. She was, after all, more than a couple of decades the man's junior and very young when the third wife passed away. What's more, being one of the silliest girls in all of England, Lydia was utterly oblivious to anything that did not directly involve her. Even with that as an excuse, Elizabeth did not mean to let Lydia eschew her responsibility for her current predicament so easily as that.

"Well then, perhaps you should have thought of

that before you decided to accept anything from the gentleman," Elizabeth said.

"Oh, Lizzy! What are you saying? Who in my position would not accept such lovely gifts? Perhaps if you had not been so miserly since Papa's passing, I would have had no need to accept Mr. Coble's presents. You know how much I like nice things!"

"In Lydia's defense, she did receive some very nice things," said Kitty, nodding her head.

"Where are these *nice* things, Lydia?" Elizabeth asked.

Kitty sprang to her feet and hurried to a large wooden trunk in the corner of the room. She threw open the lid. "Here they are!" She began rifling through the assorted garments. "Come and see for yourself, Lizzy! Are they not beautiful?" she added, holding one against her body for her sister's inspection.

"Kitty!" Lydia exclaimed. "You have no right. You know this was meant to be our secret." She scurried from the bed and tried unsuccessfully to seize the emerald-colored gown. "Give it to me!"

Elizabeth walked over to the trunk and started picking through Lydia's treasure. And what a treasure it was. Silken gowns, though not of the latest fashions, their value was patently obvious. Also included were combs, brushes, and assorted trinkets. Whiffs of bottled perfumes assaulted her senses. Elizabeth was appalled.

"Lydia, what have you done? What were you thinking? Why even you ought to have known the man would expect something in return for his generosity. But that is beside the point as I will see that everything he ever gave you is returned so soon as we can pack it all up." She slammed the lid closed with a resounding thump as a means of displaying her revulsion.

Elizabeth regarded Lydia pointedly. "Unless you want to risk being forced to wed that horrible man, you will do as I say and not breathe a word of any of this to anyone." She glared at Kitty. "The same goes for you, Kitty. This must be our secret if I am to stand a chance of extricating Lydia from this dreadful situation. Do I have your words?"

Both young ladies agreed that they would speak to no one of Mr. Coble's proposition, realizing rightly or wrongly that doing so might be the means of Lydia's death.

*Oh, to find oneself responsible for two of the silliest girls in all of England,* Elizabeth considered, even though a part of her knew that this was no trivial matter. She had no idea if her plan to return the gifts to Mr. Coble would be enough. In fact, she rather suspected it would not be. But she would be terribly remiss if she did not try.

"Now that we are in agreement regarding this secret, let us make haste in getting all these things back to Mr. Coble where they belong."

"Everything?" Lydia cried.

"Yes, everything! That is unless you indeed plan to accept the gentleman's terms, which of course, you will not. Mr. Coble is not a man to be trusted. A man of his standing who preys on the young and foolish is a low life, someone who is beneath contempt."

"La!" Lydia exclaimed. "I resent your description of me in such disparaging words as that."

"If not foolish, then what? How did you find your-self in such a position, Lydia? You are far too young to move about in the same circles as that gentleman."

"Lydia dined at Mr. Coble's home," said Kitty. "It happened when you and Mary were in Kent!"

"You did what? The man is old enough to be your father! How did you find yourself a guest at his home?"

"It was her particular friend, Mrs. Forster. She invited Lydia to accompany her and her husband, Colonel Forster, to Mr. Coble's home. That is when Lydia first caught the gentleman's notice."

Elizabeth was aware that her youngest sister was a

favorite of the young lady whom the colonel of the local militia had recently married. She had hoped the other woman would have been a good influence over Lydia. *Apparently not.*

"Yes, but it was entirely innocent. I was never alone with the gentleman, not even once."

"Oh! But what about the time you went for a ride in his carriage?" Kitty asked. "I seem to recall your saying the two of you were alone then."

The younger girl grabbed a nearby pillow and tossed it at her sibling. "Oh, hush, Kitty!" Lydia exclaimed with energy.

"No, Kitty. On the contrary," said Elizabeth. "It seems you have a far better recollection of Lydia's involvement with Mr. Coble than she does."

"No, she does not. Kitty is simply jealous. She is upset that Mrs. Forster is my particular friend, and hence she is simply telling falsehoods to discredit her."

"I am not the jealous one. You are the jealous one!" Kitty shouted.

"No! You are the jealous one. You have always been jealous of me because I am the tallest of all my sisters and the prettiest!"

"Pray, cease your silly bickering this instant. Time is of the essence! We must get rid of these things before the rest of the family returns."

*What a most unenviable position in which to find oneself,* Elizabeth was forced to concede. Were this information widely known, the Bennets' reputation would be ruined.

Mrs. Bennet's absence, as well as Mary's, proved to be a blessing. As for the former, Elizabeth was not sure her mother would not celebrate the idea of her youngest daughter getting married. She might suppose that even being forced to wed a monster would be better than not marrying at all. Elizabeth would like to think her mother would not wish to see her youngest daughter subjected to such a cruel fate, but she did not want to risk it.

As for Mr. Collins, Elizabeth feared the threat of such a scandal on the horizon would surely frighten him off. And then where would her family be? Telling Mary was not an option either, for she might be compelled to confide in her intended. Mary was much too righteous minded to do otherwise.

*No, the fewer people who know about this abominable situation, the better.*

# CHAPTER 20

*W*ithout drawing too much attention to herself, Elizabeth had made her way to Mr. Coble's home. Not wishing to be alone with him for too long, she had a loyal family servant accompany her – the same servant whom she had entrusted to pack up all the gentleman's property and bring it along.

Her conversation with the man, however, required the utmost discretion, and thus she stood in the parlor, staring him face-to-face. It was just the two of them. Her goodwill gesture had failed to impress the horrible man. His lewd manner appalled her.

"What do you mean, sir? I saw to it that everything in my sister's possession was returned," Elizabeth declared.

A tall, thin man, Coble towered over her. One who did not know him might mistake him for a proper gentleman. He looked and dressed the part. Elizabeth knew better. His shifty expression and wily voice gave him the aura of a sly fox.

Shaking his head, he said, "Not everything, I fear."

"What else is there?"

"There is a matter of the missing jewelry?"

"What jewelry?"

"It would seem your sister failed to mention that. I cannot pretend to be surprised. She would have had to confess to being a thief."

"I do not believe you. My sister may be a lot of things - young and impetuous being chief among them, but she is most certainly not a thief."

"Perhaps you ought to question her before you ascribe her such virtuousness."

Elizabeth was sure that had any jewelry been involved, Kitty would have mentioned it. Both girls swore that every gift from the gentleman had been cataloged and returned. Heaven forbid Lydia had lied. She really could not be sure of anything at that point.

"Sir, as I have said, my sister is not a thief," Elizabeth cried with as much conviction as she could muster.

"There is one way to settle this matter. I might have

the constable search your home. Imagine what your neighbors would say."

No! That would never do. Such a stratagem would surely shine a light on Lydia's foolishness. The secret she forced her younger sisters to abide by would be exposed for all the world to see. Mr. Collins would find out!

"What do you want from us, sir? Are you so determined to have my sister that you would ruin her and her entire family in order to have your way?"

He scoffed. "Your sister owes me, which effectively makes her my property. One way or another, I will be satisfied."

"I am sure a man of your stature can do far better than settle for someone like Lydia. She has no fortune, no connections. What can possibly be your reason for targeting her?" Elizabeth immediately regretted her choice of words. She meant to retract what must surely be interpreted as an accusation, but she was too late.

"I had meant to be reasonable, but in the wake of your accusation, I am no longer of a mind to do so. My offer to marry your sister is rescinded. As you said, a silly girl with no fortune or connections does not warrant such consideration. Instead, I believe I will have her as my mistress. After all, a man can only have one wife - at a time - that is to say, but he may have as many mistresses as he chooses at his disposal."

Elizabeth did not know what to say or what to do in the face of such an outlandish proposal.

"On the other hand," said Mr. Coble. "I am open to an alternative arrangement."

"I am almost afraid to ask what that might be," said Elizabeth, finding her voice.

"I will accept your own favors in place of your sister's. You are a fine woman whose worth is no doubt ten times that of your sister." He shrugged. "I will even marry you if that is your preference."

The man's bulging eyes crept all over Elizabeth, making her skin crawl.

"I am sure I would not marry you even if you were the last man in the world!" Elizabeth spat. "Sacrifice myself on the altar of my sister's folly? I think not."

He laughed in her face. "You speak too soon, Miss Elizabeth, for there is yet another bit of information for you to ponder. Instead of engaging the constable's services and thereby causing a scandal, I believe my purposes would be better served simply by going directly to Mr. William Collins. Surely he will want to know that a thief is residing under his roof - that a thief is to be his sister-in-law."

Once again, Elizabeth was at a loss for words. She

was too furious to trust herself in such a situation. Her courage always rose at every attempt to intimidate her. But not this time when everything that meant anything to her was at stake.

"It seems, I have given you much to consider, Miss Elizabeth, and so I will leave you to mull over my proposal. I have an appointment in town that I do not want to miss. However, feel free to stay and have a look around my home. If you care as much about your family's welfare as I suspect you do, I believe you will know exactly what is to be done."

---

Elizabeth did not sleep at all that night. Tossing and turning, she did not want to close her eyes, for the memory of that despicable Mr. Coble, and the disgusting way he looked at her and spoke to her kept creeping into her dreams.

Not wanting to distress her sister Jane and yet needing to confide in someone whom she could trust, Elizabeth went to Lucas Lodge early the next day.

She did not wish to be overheard, especially by Lady Lucas, who was as excitable as Elizabeth's own mother, Mrs. Bennet. Thus Elizabeth invited her intimate friend to have a walk outside in the garden as soon as she could.

Once alone, Elizabeth told Charlotte about all that had unfolded during the past couple of days. She described how Mr. Coble had threatened to ruin Lydia if she did not agree to marry him, how Lydia had foolishly embroiled herself with such a man by accepting gifts from him, and how he was now accusing the silly girl of stealing expensive jewelry from his home.

He had even threatened that Lydia need not marry him if she were entirely resolved against it—that he preferred to take her as his mistress instead.

"Oh, Charlotte," Elizabeth cried. "How is such a scandalous proposition even to be considered? Young Lydia, a girl who is not yet sixteen, the concubine of a wretched man widowed three times over - a man several decades her senior! Such a fate is not to be borne. I told him as much."

Her friend's shock in hearing this speech was just as Elizabeth had expected it to be.

Charlotte was appalled! "And then what happened?"

"I fear my efforts were utterly in vain." Elizabeth shook her head. "No! Worse than that. I fear I merely exacerbated the situation—only not for Lydia, but for myself."

"What did you do?"

Elizabeth began relaying how the man had turned the tables on her. Wringing her hands, she said, "Mr. Coble has declared that he will absolve Lydia of her so-called offenses, but only if I will substitute myself for her. I have thought long and hard about this, and I fear I have no choice other than to agree to his despicable scheme. I must marry him myself."

Charlotte gasped! "I cannot see why you would even consider sacrificing yourself at the altar of Lydia's stupidity. I am not saying the situation is not dreadful in every sense of the word. But it is Lydia's own doing, is it not?"

"Oh, if it were only that simple. Lydia is a fool, and her ignorance and caprice blinded her. She was bound to make our family ridiculous. She only wanted the opportunity."

Charlotte nodded. "Those are my sentiments exactly. Lydia very well ought to reap what she has sown."

"Again, if only it were as simple as that. However, it is not. Lydia's stupidity does not relieve me of the responsibility my father left me. I ought to have done more to keep Lydia under good regulation. Then, she might never have garnered that vile Mr. Coble's notice. What a despicable wretch! He does not deserve to exist in civilized society."

"That is all the more reason for you to steer clear of him. You ought not to underestimate the danger in dealing with such a man. If nothing else, you ought to tell your uncle Mr. Phillips about Mr. Coble's threats."

"No!" Elizabeth cried. "I fear the surest way of having the scandal exposed is to go to my uncle - either of them."

"But why?"

"Doing so would cause a fate that I deem even worse than my marrying that vile man. Mr. Coble has threatened to go to Mr. Collins if I do not do as he says. From what I know and suspect of Mr. Collins, he would not wish to align himself with a family embroiled in scandal. He is now the master of Longbourn. He will toss my mother, my sisters, and me into the hedgerows."

"You cannot know that for sure."

"I know I dare not risk it." Elizabeth covered her face with both hands, wanting to rid her mind of this picture of her family. Resuming her speech, she said, "Mary's happiness, which is all but assured, will be snatched away from her. Then there is Jane to consider and her budding relationship with Mr. Bingley. You know his pernicious sisters too well to suppose they would allow their brother to align himself with a disgraced family. They can barely countenance his affection for my sister as it is."

By now, Elizabeth had spent enough time with both ladies to know that of which she spoke.

*Miss Bingley's disdain is always on display, and Mrs. Hurst's indifference is barely disguised.*

"Oh! Charlotte, this is dreadful. Either my family will be destitute, and Mary and Jane will be heartbroken, or I will spend the rest of my life imprisoned in a loveless marriage - the fourth wife of a nefarious scoundrel, or far worse. One who preys on the young and the helpless."

"I suppose I understand your reason for not telling your uncles about the man's threats, given all that is at stake, but it is not as though you are entirely without protection."

"What do you mean, Charlotte?"

"Mr. Darcy is not a man without means. What would be the harm in confiding in him?"

"No, I do not dare say a word to him. What am I to tell him? That once again, I face the possibility of marrying a man whom I do not love–cannot love–for the sake of my family? That unless I commit to Mr. Coble's scheme, he will subject my family to destitution with no place to go and a reputation in shambles?

"I do not know that his good opinion of me would not suffer a severe blow if he knew what I am contemplating. No, I dare not say a word of this to him. That goes for you too, Charlotte. You are not to breathe a word of what I have confided to you to Mr. Darcy. This is our secret."

"Not breathe a word to me about what?"

Both ladies turned in unison. Mr. Darcy himself stood not four feet away.

"Mr. Darcy!"

# CHAPTER 21

"What must you be thinking in, once again, placing your own happiness at risk for the sake of your family?"

And this was his response? This is what Mr. Darcy felt most compelled to say after listening to Elizabeth pour her heart out to him about her family's dire situation and her plans for extricating them and thereby mitigating the disaster.

"Sir, you cannot tell me that were you in my place that you would not do the same for your family."

"What I can tell you is that, in this case, you do not have to make such a sacrifice. There are other means of dealing with men of Coble's ilk."

"How is such a man to be worked on? We have no fortune, no connections, indeed nothing to persuade him to abandon his evil scheme. I do not dare involve my uncles, who, no doubt, would seek legal remedy, for I fear the law is on that scoundrel's side.

"In a court of law, as well as the court of public opinion, it would be his word against Lydia's. And if I am honest," Elizabeth added in a yet more agitated voice, "even I cannot be certain of my sister's innocence—not after what she has done. My family's reputation would be ruined!"

"You are mistaken, Miss Elizabeth. You may be without fortune, but you are certainly not without connections."

"Pray, you are not speaking of Mr. Collins? From what I know of him, he will do anything but allow his own name to be tarnished. He will break the engagement with my sister in a heartbeat, and who would blame him?" She burst into tears as she alluded to it, and for a few seconds, could not speak another word.

His voice pained on Elizabeth's behalf, Mr. Darcy said, "In saying you are not without connections, I was thinking only of myself. I can intervene on your behalf. I can be the one you need at such a time as this when you need it most. Let me do your bidding."

Elizabeth held up her hand. "No, I cannot allow it."

"Why in heavens not?" Mr. Darcy asked, his

expression as well as his tone evidencing a measure of exasperation.

"How could I possibly expect you to involve yourself in this matter? You who are so wholly unconnected to my family and me, especially when I refuse to go to either of them?"

"At the risk of sounding immodest, I have immeasurable means the likes of which your family cannot even fathom. Coble will come to know I am the last man in the world he would wish to cross."

He drew closer to Elizabeth. "I know your heart is in the right place, and your intentions for your family are good. I fear you have suffered a burden which no one in your situation ought to have endured. Not that you are wanting or that you lack true grit, strength, and determination. You are not yet one and twenty, and yet you are expected to protect a mother as well as four sisters – sisters whose ages are approximately the same as your own. Worst of all, your best efforts have always been hampered by the fact that your home is entailed away from the female line, placing all of you at the mercy of a stranger until recently."

"And unless my sister marries Mr. Collins and until they beget a male heir, my family's situation will remain tenuous," Elizabeth reminded her companion. "As hopeless as it may seem to you, the burden of protecting my family is my fate. My father entrusted the responsibility to me. I will not forsake his memory."

"No one expects you to forsake your father's memory, Miss Elizabeth. But surely, your late father would not have expected you to forsake your happiness. I will not allow you to forsake your happiness, not so long as it is within my power to affect a solution far better than is currently expected."

"As tempting as it is to surrender my burdens to you, sir, I do not know that I can."

"Is this your final resolve?"

"I fear I have no choice."

"You always have a choice."

"Then, I choose to absolve you from this entire sordid affair. I know what I must do."

"Then, I will leave you to it," he declared, with more feeling than politeness. Collecting himself, he said, "Good day, Miss Elizabeth. I, too, know what I must do."

"What does that even mean, Mr. Darcy?"

"Do you trust me, Miss Elizabeth? I mean really trust me?"

Tears pooled in her eyes. She nodded.

He took her hands in his. "Then trust me."

Men of Jerrod Coble's ilk were Darcy's abhorrence. A man of sense and education with knowledge of the world, Darcy had met more than a few such men in his business dealings as well as in his personal life.

While listening to Elizabeth explaining her dilemma with Coble owing chiefly to her sister, the recollection of a harrowing incident with his former friend and now his worst enemy, George Wickham, immediately came to mind.

Taking advantage of unsuspecting young girls was Wickham's *modus operandi*. Darcy's own sister, Georgiana, had nearly fallen prey to Wickham's ploy to elope with him so he could gain control of her inheritance of thirty thousand pounds.

At age fifteen, Georgiana's life would have been ruined. Darcy's unexpected, yet timely, arrival in Ramsgate put an end to the scheme, for when he made it clear to George Wickham that he would never see a penny of his sister's inheritance, the scandal scurried off to parts unknown.

Darcy supposed rather than knew that Wickham was hiding under some rock in town. He could not care less whether his supposition was correct. What he had done, though, was take precautions to make sure

Wickham would never pose a threat to his sister again by secretly buying the scoundrel's debts, which amounted to more than a few thousand pounds. Unbeknown to Wickham, should he ever cross Darcy again, the latter would know precisely how to act.

*In hindsight, taking care of George Wickham was easy. But what of Jerrod Coble? How on earth is this man to be worked on?*

Before parting with Elizabeth, Darcy had asked her not to do anything rash. In the state she was in, he could not be sure she would heed his advice.

*When it comes to protecting her family, Elizabeth heeds her own counsel, even at her own detriment.*

She had effectively claimed her youngest sister's perils as her own and all for the sake of her family's reputation and their security.

Having never met Elizabeth's late father, Darcy could not help but question the man's judgment. Was it not enough that despite Elizabeth's best intentions, her hands would forever be tied, owing to the circumstances of the entail?

*Now is not the time to pass judgment on a man whom I knew nothing about, nor is it time to ponder what might have been.*

All his time and attention must be focused on the problem at hand – working on the vile Mr. Coble.

*Even the most powerful of men have their Achilles heel – a particular weakness capable of leading to their downfall. Be it greed, a shady past, skeletons hidden away in a closet, insurmountable gambling debts, or worse. Whatever is Coble's vice, I must do everything in my power to unearth it.*

*The alternative of Elizabeth bending to that vile man's will is not an option.*

Darcy supposed his friend Charles Bingley, having settled in his new home weeks ahead of Darcy's arrival, seemed the logical first step in the quest to ascertain who Jerrod Coble was and what he was all about. Actually, engaging his London solicitors by way of an urgent express was the first order of business. Having done that, Darcy sat across from Bingley in the drawing-room at Netherfield.

"Darcy, it seems out of character for you to express such a keen interest in someone like Mr. Coble. Might I ask what this is about? Does it involve matters of business?"

He nodded. "You might say that. Pray, what do you know about his character?"

"Very little, I am afraid. He is one of the few gentlemen who has not called on Netherfield to introduce himself, as so many others have done. I would say he does not easily recommend himself to strangers. On the other hand, he is known to dine regularly with the officers. He has had them at his home on many occasions, or so I have heard. I believe he may be a bit of a gamester. Of course, I am merely speculating. Should I make a concerted effort to discover more about him?"

Darcy shook his head. "No, that will not be necessary. In fact, say nothing of anything to anyone about my interest in this man. For now, I must not show my hand."

"Of course. You may rely upon my discretion," Bingley replied. Changing the subject, he continued, "That being said, there is a matter which I wish to discuss with you. It has to do with Miss Bennet."

"Miss Bennet," Darcy said, his first thought being of Elizabeth. Always Elizabeth.

Bingley nodded. "Miss Jane Bennet."

Darcy released his breath. Of course, Bingley was speaking of Jane. *In fact, he often speaks of the eldest Bennet sister.*

Darcy leaned forward. "What is it you wish to say?"

"Well—I know I may have said this before, but this time I really mean it. At least, I think I do. I know I want to." Bingley combed his fingers through his hair. "I – I—"

"You what?"

"I am in love with her," Bingley explained. He bolted to his feet and started pacing. "However, I fear she does not return my feelings."

Darcy sat there in silence, his heart going out to his friend. What could he say? What could he do? He, too, had observed his friend and Miss Jane Bennet together on several occasions since his arrival in Hertfordshire. Several times the gentlemen had called at Longbourn. They even took a family dinner with the Bennets. They also had been in company with the Bennets at a couple of the other neighboring estates for dinner.

True, Miss Bennet smiled a lot whenever she was engaged in discussion with Bingley, but other than that, Darcy had seen no evidence of any real affection.

"Darcy," he said, "did you not hear me?"

"Pray, forgive me, Bingley. What are you asking?"

"Do you suppose it is merely Caroline's repeated disparagement of the Bennets that have made me doubt my own opinion? If so, I am asking for yours. Do you agree with my sister that any feelings Miss Bennet may have for me are rooted in her desire to do what is in the best interest of her family and nothing more?"

# CHAPTER 22

*D*arcy's determined pursuit of Mr. Coble found him back in London because that is where the latter had gone. Coble's being in town eased Darcy's troubled mind, for so long as the scoundrel was in London, he was away from Elizabeth and her family. For now, the Bennets, and especially Elizabeth, were safe.

Even in London, Darcy's conversation with his friend Bingley kept creeping into his mind when least expected. What a conundrum for his young friend. What a conundrum for Darcy.

He knew enough to know that the Bennet sisters fiercely protected their own, even at the expense of their own individual happiness. This was undoubtedly true of Elizabeth. He had no reason to suppose Miss

Jane Bennet's motives did not mirror her sister's. Complicating Darcy's situation, even more, were his own feelings for Elizabeth.

*I have fallen in love with Elizabeth. And yet, she acts as though she does not know it. How can she consider marrying a man out of fear of retribution against her family when all the love I have for her is right here?*

*Have my sentiments not been on full display? Have I not shown Elizabeth the depth of my feelings for her through my actions, even if not in so many words?*

By now, Darcy had gathered enough knowledge about Mr. Coble to wage a campaign to spare the Bennets from the man's evil scheme. Darcy's solicitors arranged a face-to-face meeting between the two gentlemen purportedly for purposes of business.

They met at White's.

Seated at a table ideally suited to their purposes, Darcy's desire to conclude their business demanded that they commence negotiations before they finished the first round of drinks.

"Now that you know who I am," Darcy said, tacitly acknowledging that his solicitors' investigations of Coble had encouraged the latter to make inquiries of his own, "the unseemly matter between you and the Bennet family is at its end."

Taken aback, Coble reared his head. "I beg your

pardon. What do my affairs with the Bennets have to do with this supposed business arrangement we are here to discuss?"

"The cessation of your 'dealings' with the Bennets is the business arrangement at hand. I am prepared to be very generous. Indeed, here is my offer," said Darcy, retrieving a slip of paper from his pocket. He slid it, face down, to Coble's side of the table.

Wasting no time, Coble seized it. The man almost gasped aloud. His menacing eyes bulged.

Mr. Darcy said nothing.

Coble broke the silence. Rubbing his chin, he asked, "Mind if I ask what these Bennets are to you? A man of your standing does not offer this much on behalf of a penniless lot of ninnies with no connections, no fortunes, and nothing to recommend themselves."

Darcy leaned in. "My interest in this matter can be nothing to you. Take the money and be satisfied knowing that your future will be far more enhanced in having done so."

Coble scoffed. "That sounds like a threat."

Darcy shrugged. "Take it as a threat or a promise. The end result will be the same. If you refuse my offer, I will exercise every means at my disposal to ruin you. As it stands now, you are nothing to me."

Pushing his chair away from the table, Darcy stood. "Let us keep it that way." He nodded. "I shall expect to hear from you before too long."

---

Not long after Darcy quit the establishment, a tall man who had been sitting with a rather respectable-looking gentleman at another table across the room sauntered over to where Coble sat.

"Do you mind if I join you?" the man asked.

Coble looked up from the paper he was still studying. With that amount of money, all his troubles would be over. What a tempting offer indeed.

"Do I know you, sir?" Coble asked.

"Not yet, but you will want to know me, I am sure. It appears we share a mutual acquaintance. And judging by the manner of your former drinking partner's abrupt departure, he is no fonder of you than he is of me."

No doubt taking Coble's silence as encouragement, the tall gentleman sat in the chair Darcy had abandoned and held out his hand. "I am George Wickham - at your service."

Elizabeth may have been at Longbourn in body, but hardly in spirit. Her busy mind was thoroughly engaged in unknowing and conjecture.

Mr. Darcy returned to London. The last Elizabeth had heard, Mr. Coble was away too. Is it too much to hope Coble is lying face down in a ditch alongside a lonely country road?

Elizabeth never wished to cause anyone harm. But if she had the power to make wishes come true, she would not be in her current predicament.

*My beloved father would be alive.*

*There would be no entail on our home.*

*My sister Jane would see.*

Her wish that the one man who would be her greatest enemy was dead amounted to nothing.

Elizabeth's busy mind continued racing. *Is that scoundrel in town? Does Mr. Darcy's being in town have anything to do with Mr. Coble's absence from Hertfordshire?*

Whatever the reason for the man's absence, one thing was clear. His being away gave Elizabeth a much-needed reprieve, even if it was temporary.

Elizabeth buried herself in the book she received in Kent. With the turn of each page, she fought the urge to think of the gentleman who gave it to her and wonder what might have been.

Darcy had surely expected to hear from Coble, but it somewhat surprised him to know the man had come to his home. After telling his butler to show the man into his study, Darcy sat at his large mahogany desk and waited. He would not stand. Coble did not deserve such a courtesy.

"That did not take long." Darcy gestured toward an empty chair, inviting the visitor to sit. "No doubt you are here to accept my offer in person."

"Not exactly," Coble replied, crossing one leg over the other. "Your offer is tempting, but I have since learned that it is hardly a sacrifice for a man of your means. I now feel rather insulted, knowing what I know."

Darcy scoffed. "I am certain we both know things, Coble."

"True, true. Let me just say I know more now than I did when we sat across from each other at White's. From what I am told, keeping this new information from seeing the light of day is worth far more than this pittance." Here, he crumbled the slip of paper Darcy had handed him earlier and threw it. It landed atop Darcy's desk.

"You are a bigger fool than I thought, turning up

your nose on such a bounty, and based on what? Some supposed new information that you think you can use against me?"

"I believe I would be a fool were I to accept your first offer, albeit a generous one, made to preserve the reputation of the Bennet sisters when the reputation of your own sister is at stake, would I not?"

Darcy rose from his chair. "My sister!" His eyes shot daggers at the man. "You dare to mention my sister. You know nothing about her."

"On the contrary. I knew nothing about her when I entered White's. But by the time I quit the establishment, I had learned quite a bit about the young lady, as well as her dowry of thirty thousand pounds."

The man did not need to say more. The earlier suspicion Darcy had suffered that his nemesis George Wickham was sulking about in the shadows at White's, he had dismissed thinking it merely a figment of his imagination.

Coble sitting across from him and smirking, no less, said it all.

"You have made a grievous mistake in coming here, Coble. Indeed, instead of being nothing to me as I had hoped you would be, you have placed yourself in grave danger of being my worst enemy.

"You know your own vices as well as I do. Three

dead wives warrant more than mere cursory investigations, do they not? I have the means to pursue the truth to the ends of the earth. Do not give me the motive!"

Darcy retrieved the crumpled paper from his desk and hurled it at Coble's face. "Accept my one and only offer and walk away!"

# CHAPTER 23

*F*inding his nemesis was easy enough, for where else would he be but in the general proximity of a Mrs. Younge, the woman who had been in charge of Darcy's sister during the Ramsgate incident.

Getting the woman to betray her cohort's whereabouts did not take much effort. Now, it was Darcy's turn to sit opposite George Wickham, but in an establishment not quite so exclusive as White's. The smoked-filled air, the stench of cheap liquor, and the steady roar of laughter and foul language occupied every corner of the room. Darcy could hardly think a month's ablution enough to cleanse him from its impurities but dealing with Wickham must be done.

"What brings you here?" Wickham asked, his

expression as though Darcy was the last person whom he expected to see that evening.

Darcy glared at his former friend. George Wickham's vile propensities always rendered him unworthy of polite society, but never before had Darcy recalled the man's general appearance being so wanting. No wonder he did not recognize him earlier at White's.

"Well, do not just stand there looking stupid," Wickham said. "Pull up a chair, old man. Let us have a round of drinks - on you, of course."

"I did not come all this way to have drinks, you fool."

"Is that any way to greet an old friend?"

Darcy scoffed. "An old friend? There may have been a time when we were friends. But you are nothing to me now."

"Then why are you here?" Wickham picked up the empty canister on his table and tried to drain the very last drop into his equally empty glass. "No, let me guess. Might your being here have anything to do with our new friend?" He toppled the empty canister on its side. "What was his name? Oh yes! Mr. Coble of Hertfordshire." He laughed a little. "What business can you possibly have in Hertfordshire? Not that it matters to me. All I know is the man owes me quite a hefty sum,

by now. I can hardly wait to get what's coming to me."
Wickham hiccupped.

Darcy rolled his eyes. Wickham was so deep in his cups that Darcy wondered if he should simply give up on the fool.

*No, it will not do. I need to settle this matter with Wickham once and for all.*

Summoning a nearby waiter, Darcy demanded a jug of water be brought to the table. Not long after its arrival, he threw most of its contents into Wickham's face.

Being drenched in cold water proved rather sobering - at least enough so to alert Wickham to his senses.

"Listen to me, you fool," Darcy declared. "You had better locate this *so-called* friend of yours and retract everything you said about what happened last summer."

George Wickham huffed. "And what if I do not? You do not frighten me with all your fancy airs and meaningless threats. I know you!"

"Then you know that I do not make idle threats. If you value your freedom, you will do as I say. Did you really expect I would sit idly by and hope and pray you would never betray me further after what happened?"

Though Wickham's scheme was directed at young

Miss Darcy, Darcy was convinced that harming Georgiana was not Wickham's chief goal. He really meant to hurt Darcy himself.

"I will see you rot in jail before I allow you to harm my family or me ever again."

Wickham's mouth twitched. "Jail?" he balked, still wiping water from his face. "I have done nothing that warrants being locked away!"

"Nothing except amass significant debts from here to Derbyshire. I know it all - the gambling, the swindling of unsuspecting merchants. I know it all because I have covered it all. I own your debts, which means I own you."

Darcy threw a disgusted glance about the room. He glared at Wickham. "I am only thankful that my father cannot see you. He would never have believed you capable of sinking so low. Of course, you and I both knew better."

"Your father - my godfather - never meant for me to suffer so in life. We both know who is to blame for my current predicament. Had you only granted me the living in Kympton that ought to have been mine—"

Darcy rolled his eyes. "I have heard it all before. Pray, give it a rest, for if you think your situation is dire now, imagine how it would be were you locked away in a dark cell."

What must have been about a week later, Elizabeth sat across from her intimate friend, Charlotte. The agony she suffered the last time they were together was gone. "Mr. Coble has recanted his scurrilous allegations against my sister Lydia!"

"How wonderful! This means you are no longer in danger from that vile man."

"Oh! It is indeed wonderful. And now that the banns have been read, Mr. Collins and Mary are to be married. I could not have wished for a better outcome."

"Let us pray that Lydia has learned a lesson, and she will do no harm in the meantime."

"To be sure. I have threatened to throw her in Mr. Coble's way if she even bats an eye at another man before Mary's wedding."

"Good for you, Lizzy."

"It is positively amazing the fear of being forced to wed the 'merry' widower has over such a silly girl. Even I am surprised that she and Kitty kept their silence this entire time."

"Poor Lydia must be miserable."

"It serves her right. But she is young. She will, no doubt, be back to her old ways before the wedding breakfast ends, at which point our family will be obliged to lock her away forever."

No doubt desiring to change the subject, Charlotte said, "What of Mr. Darcy? Does he remain in town?"

"I believe he does," Elizabeth said. "And I will not deny my being concerned about his absence.

"I have not the slightest doubt that I have him to thank for Mr. Coble's about-face. Were Mr. Darcy here, I might at least thank him. I can only imagine to what lengths he must have gone to ensure a happier outcome than would have otherwise been possible."

"Fear not, dearest Lizzy. No doubt, it is only a matter of time before Mr. Darcy returns. A man does not go to such lengths solely to be of service to a damsel in distress. I am sure he is in love with you."

This was not the first time that Charlotte had made allusions along a similar vein about Mr. Darcy's affection for Elizabeth. Only this time, Elizabeth was not so quick to dismiss her friend's supposition.

"If only it were so, Charlotte. For the first time in my life, I have come to know how much I could have loved such a man. Leave it to me to come to such a realization when all hope must surely be in vain."

Elizabeth indeed had a reason for doubt, for the Netherfield party had recently left Hertfordshire. Mr. Bingley had gone to London not too long ago, taking with him Jane's best chance of strengthening their acquaintance and leaving behind a vague promise of his return.

His sisters' departure almost immediately afterward, no doubt, was meant to put an end to all of Jane's hopes, for a letter was delivered to Longbourn with words to that effect later that very day.

Had they found out about the Bennet family's impending doom? Was Lydia's shame fodder for the Netherfield party's further derision? The final nail in the coffin sealing Jane's fate?

Elizabeth could not rightly say, and if Mr. Darcy, too, had decided that the risk of his continuing acquaintance outweighed any possible rewards, Elizabeth could not rightly say that she blamed him.

"Your hopes for a future with Mr. Darcy are not in vain," Charlotte cried. "Do not dare allow such despair to fester in your mind."

"But it has been days since Mr. Coble abandoned his pursuit."

"What is such a short passage of time in the overall scheme of things? Mr. Darcy will return. Of that, I have no doubt. And when he does, you must not delay. You must seize the happiness that surely awaits you, and hold on to it for the rest of your life."

# CHAPTER 24

When Mr. Darcy returned to Hertfordshire, he along with his friend Bingley went directly to Longbourn. Sitting in the parlor surrounded by chattering women and engaging in polite, meaningless conversation was certainly not what he wanted to do.

Mr. Darcy had but one thing on his mind, and that was being alone with Elizabeth. With what delight did he suffer when Mrs. Bennet and Miss Mary excused themselves to oversee the final wedding preparations, and the younger ladies went for a walk to Meryton with errands of their own.

Only Jane and Mr. Bingley and Elizabeth and Mr. Darcy remained in the parlor. Now it was Mr. Darcy who was the one to suggest a turn in the garden. The latter couple allowed the former to outpace them, and when they came upon a fork in the path, Mr. Darcy coaxed Elizabeth to follow his lead.

They walked and walked, and soon the garden in which Jane and Bingley had taken a seat was nowhere in sight. The silence that had accompanied them most of the way was broken when Elizabeth broached the subject of what had happened with Mr. Coble.

Mr. Darcy began speaking on the matter, sharing what he could and omitting what he felt he could not.

Elizabeth listened. She spoke very little, and when he concluded his speech, she said, "Other than my undying gratitude, what do I now owe you after what you have done for my family, sir?"

"Surely you must know you owe me nothing."

"But I can scarcely imagine the expense you must have incurred to bend that evil man to your will."

Thinking it only fair to relieve Elizabeth of the burden she suffered, Darcy confided in her his own family secret. He told her of Miss Darcy's near brush with scandal the summer before, how Coble had learned of it, and how the villain had attempted to use it against him.

This information seemed to ease Elizabeth's mind, and despite the compassion such a confession must surely evoke, she did not press him further on the matter.

Now, she was silent again. Too silent for his liking. He told her as much, which was sufficient encouragement for Elizabeth to speak on a different subject.

"Sir, I am a curious creature, and as you ought to know by now, my frankness of character demands satisfaction."

"What is at the heart of your assertion?"

"Well - I fear I would be terribly remiss if I did not ask you about your feelings regarding your friend Mr. Bingley and my sister Jane."

"I will not deny that my friend's feelings for your sister are strong - such that I have never witnessed before, and I must confess to being more than a little concerned."

"Why is that, if I may ask?" Without waiting for a reply, she added, "Is it my family's want of connections, our lack of fortune? I ask because neither of those things is a great secret and yet Mr. Bingley does not seem to be bothered."

"No, it is just that he is of an age where his connections are constantly increasing. He is only just coming into his own. There is so much of the world he has yet to experience."

"Do you feel an alliance with my sister will hinder

his prospects? Again, Mr. Bingley must have considered that as well."

"If I am to be completely forthcoming about my concerns—"

"Please do," Elizabeth interrupted.

"I have observed the two of them most closely, and I fear your sister's attachment to Bingley is not so strong as his attachment to her. All things considered, an equal degree of affection ought to exist if nothing else."

"What if I were to tell you that my sister rarely shares her true feelings with anyone?"

"I dare not argue with you. You know your sister best."

"Surely you can understand the reason my sister does not wear her most heartfelt sentiments on her sleeve?"

"Are you suggesting she is unsure of herself and what she might add to a possible alliance? That she would rather do anything but subject her heart to agony and pain?"

"I suppose," Elizabeth said tentatively. "Surely you must comprehend her reasoning."

"What of your own reasoning, Miss Elizabeth? Are you afraid of subjecting yourself to possible heartbreak and pain as well?"

"We are not talking about me, Mr. Darcy. In broaching this topic, I believe I am thinking only of my sister."

"I say it is time you stop thinking only of your sister, rather sisters, and start thinking of yourself."

"What are you saying, Mr. Darcy?"

"Miss Elizabeth," he began, "have my feelings toward you been so muted - my intentions so unclear?

"I love you, most ardently. You have bewitched me from the moment I first laid eyes on you. I recall telling you in Kent you must never hesitate in reaching out to me.

"During your moment of crisis, I asked you to place your trust in me, and you did. Your doing so meant the world to me. Now, I have something more to ask. Will you continue to place your trust in me? More than that, will you let me spend the rest of my life with you? Loving you?"

Elizabeth's warm smile encouraged Mr. Darcy to draw nearer. "What I truly mean to say is, will you marry me? Will you be my wife?"

Elizabeth said yes.

*She said yes!*

And she further added that her sentiments were as ardent as were his, even if bewildered more aptly described the moment she first laid eyes on him. But love him, she did, without even knowing precisely when she had made a start. She supposed she was in the middle of loving him before she even knew she had begun.

Every look, every word, and every second Darcy and Elizabeth ever shared had led to that moment, and he expressed himself on the occasion as sensibly and as warmly as a man violently in love was meant to do.

*Our first kiss.*

Elizabeth's response, so innocent and yet so passionate, was everything he dreamed it would be - promising him of all the pleasures between the two of them yet to come.

# EPILOGUE

*H*appy for all her maternal feelings was the day Mrs. Bennet's third daughter, Mary, became the new mistress of Longbourn. Mary, the one daughter whom she feared the least likely to find a husband, was the first of her daughters to do so.

The happiness that was hers grew three times over soon after the newly wedded Mr. and Mrs. Collins drew away in their carriage headed to Brighton, the first destination of their wedding journey, and it was time for Elizabeth's as well as Jane's closely held secrets to be revealed.

Elizabeth was engaged to marry Mr. Darcy, and Jane was engaged to marry Mr. Bingley.

Oh! What a happy day indeed.

Soon enough, Mrs. Bennet boasted of having three

sons-in-law. She could think of no one more deserving of such an honor than herself.

Elizabeth really loved Mr. Darcy, and she loved him even more, suspecting, as she did, that reassuring words from him had been the impetus his friend Bingley needed to declare himself to Jane. In doing so, the younger man had defied the most ardent wish of his sisters, especially Miss Caroline Bingley's. That did not, however, stop her from expecting a place at his table.

By design, Elizabeth rarely spent time in the company of the Bingley sisters. Her marriage to Mr. Darcy was destined to change that. Miss Bingley, especially, was very deeply mortified by Darcy's marriage, but wishing to retain the right of visiting at Pemberley, she wisely chose to keep all her resentments to herself.

Jane and Mr. Bingley remained at Netherfield. This arrangement, although not always so desirable to his easy temperament owing to the proximity of his dear wife's relations, proved infinitely desirable to Jane's affectionate heart, for it allowed her to be near her dear friend, Charlotte. Jane's happiness was Bingley's happiness, and thus he would never have any cause to repine.

And although Elizabeth would have loved being

the one to behold the joy in her dearest sister's face when Jane began to distinguish various shades of light and, albeit vaguely, some shapes, reading Charlotte's regular accounts of Jane's improvements was the next best thing to being there.

Some mention of Mr. Coble ought to be made, if only for the peace of mind which settled over Meryton with the gentleman's leave-taking. He was said to have been bound for the Americas. What was more, there had been some talk of a shipwreck. Whatever was the truth, nobody could be bothered to find out.

In choosing to defy Lady Catherine de Bourgh, by marrying the third Bennet daughter, Mr. Collins was forever to be a stranger to the grand lady. Her ladyship had promised to extend the same courtesy, or rather lack thereof, to her own nephew Darcy. His marriage was the source of extreme anger and resentment, and she told him as much in her reply to the letter which announced its arrangement. She sent him language so abusive, especially of Elizabeth, that for some time all intercourse was at an end.

Alas, it was not to last. Instead, her ladyship proclaimed that life was too short to dwell on that which would never be - a resolve that brought her to Pemberley more often than Elizabeth would have otherwise preferred.

She could not help but suspect that Lady Catherine's real purpose in coming was driven by her motive to prove that which she desired most - that Mr. Darcy would rue the day he chose such a lowly woman to be the mistress of his home.

What did Elizabeth care? Defying the wishes of Lady Catherine de Bourgh was, after all, precisely what Elizabeth had always set out to do.

Much had been mentioned about Miss Georgiana Darcy. It must be said that one of the brightest parts of Elizabeth and Mr. Darcy's season of courtship was the former's meeting the young lady. The occasion was just as formidable for one as it was for the other. Elizabeth could not be sure that had she and Mr. Darcy met under different circumstances, she would not have believed him capable of the same haughtiness so evident in his aunt Lady Catherine de Bourgh. With what pleasure did Elizabeth see that Georgiana was nothing at all like her aunt. There was sense and good humor in the younger woman's face, and her manners were perfectly unassuming and gentle.

For Darcy's part, the attachment of the sisters was exactly what he had hoped to see. Adding to his pleasure was the mutual decision between all the parties involved that Pemberley was also to be Georgiana's home. The frequent presence of Elizabeth's younger sisters, Kitty and Lydia, would surely have posed a great trial on Darcy's forbearance, were it not for the strict supervision of Mrs. Annesley, the lady in charge of his sister, especially whenever the youngest was around.

Elizabeth's frequent presence in town during the courtship period also allowed her to make up for not spending time with her uncle and aunt, Mr. and Mrs. Gardiner, when she was otherwise engaged in securing the future of Longbourn for her family. The span of an hour spent in the company of the engaged couple was more than enough to persuade them that Mr. Darcy was overflowing with admiration for their niece. And it was with a warm heart that Elizabeth embraced her aunt's commendation of her intended.

"There is something pleasing about his mouth when he speaks," Mrs. Gardiner had declared. "And there is something of dignity in his countenance that would not give one an unfavorable idea of his heart."

Having won Mr. Darcy's heart long before even she knew it, Elizabeth could not agree more.

Elizabeth's first sighting of Pemberley had taken her breath away, and the thought of what it must be like to be mistress of such a place could not help but occupy her mind. Were it not for the fact that she was cradled in Mr. Darcy's arms, she no doubt would have been perched on the edge of her seat. From her vantage point inside the luxurious carriage, every twist and turn in the lane leading to the manor house promised endless possibilities for exploration.

The journey she had embarked upon was such that she had never imagined for herself, but she was sure that if her beloved father had lived to see how her life had unfolded, he would smile and say, it was exactly the way her life was meant to be.

―――――――

One evening, long after the sun had set over Pemberley, Darcy and Elizabeth sat on the balcony enjoying the cool night's air. As much as she was enjoying the moment, Elizabeth tried to slip away from her husband's tender embrace.

"Where are you going, my love? I thought you intended for the two of us to act out the dream you were having when I came across you at the temple all those months ago. Heaven knows I have waited long enough," he murmured, combing his fingers through her long, dark hair.

Ah, Elizabeth's dream. Unbeknown to her lover, she often recalled that very dream. Their frequent interludes as man and wife exceeded her every expectation. Her earliest dream of Mr. Darcy lingered still.

*Her stepping out of the bath just as he entered her room. Her bathing gown clinging to every inch of her body. His coming to her in all his magnificent glory. His lifting her into his arms. His carrying her off to bed.*

"Oh," Elizabeth said, "I have every intention of our acting out that particular dream, my love. In doing so, my first order of business is to draw a steamy, hot bath."

Expecting His Proposal

Pride and Sensuality

A Tender Moment

Almost Persuaded

---

**Series**

*Everything Will Change*

Lady Elizabeth

So Far Away

*Dearest, Loveliest Elizabeth*

Dearest Elizabeth

Loveliest Elizabeth

Dearest, Loveliest Elizabeth

*A Darcy and Elizabeth Love Affair*

A Lasting Love Affair

'Tis the Season for Matchmaking

*Pride and Prejudice Untold*

To Have His Cake (and Eat it Too)

What He Would Not Do

Lady Harriette

*Darcy and the Young Knight's Quest*

He Taught Me to Hope

The Mission

Hope and Sensibility

Visit http://podixon.com for more.

**P. O. Dixon** is a writer as well as an entertainer. Historical England and its days of yore fascinate her. She, in particular, loves the Regency period with its strict mores and oh so proper decorum. Her ardent appreciation of Jane Austen's timeless works set her on the writer's journey.

## CONNECT WITH THE AUTHOR

Twitter: @podixon
Facebook: facebook.com/podixon
Website: podixon.com
Newsletter: bit.ly/SuchHappyNews
Email: podixon@podixon.com

Printed in Poland
by Amazon Fulfillment
Poland Sp. z o.o., Wrocław